The Illustrated
LIBRARY OF ROMANCE.

LIFE OF

Jack Sheppard

The Housebreaker;

BY

"BLUESKIN."

BEING A FAITHFUL ACCOUNT OF HIS "BIRTH, PARENTAGE, AND
EDUCATION," WITH FULL PARTICULARS OF HIS CAREER,

FROM HIS

FIRST THEFT

DOWN TO HIS

EXECUTION AT TYBURN:

INTERSPERSED WITH INTERESTING ANECDOTES OF HIS

AMOUR WITH EDGEWORTH BESS;

AND PARTICULAR DESCRIPTIONS OF HIS

CELEBRATED ESCAPES.

THE PRINCIPAL INCIDENTS ARE ILLUSTRATED BY

SPLENDID LITHOGRAPHIC DRAWINGS;

ONE OF WHICH WILL BE GIVEN WITH EACH NUMBER.

GLOVER, PUBLISHER, WATER LANE, FLEET STREET, LONDON.

FROST AND VINCENT,

THE WELSH CHARTIST LEADERS.

ACCURATE LIKENESSES OF THESE POPULAR MEN,

taken from life during the sittings of the " Convention" in London, are published in a series of

PORTRAITS OF THE PEOPLE'S FRIENDS,

Comprising, amongst others,

REV. J. R. STEPHENS,	DOCTOR JOHN TAYLOR,
RICHARD OASTLER, (the Old King!)	ROBERT OWEN, &c., &c., &c.

Proofs on Imperial Paper, 6d. ; Small Paper, 3d.

Also, a beautiful group of

FIVE PORTRAITS ON ONE SHEET;

RICHARD OASTLER,	BRONTERRE O'BRIEN,
FEARGUS O'CONNOR,	HENRY HUNT,

WILLIAM COBBETT.

Price 2d. only.   Proof Impressions, 6d.

ALFRED CARLILE, PUBLISHER, WATER LANE, FLEET STREET. LONDON.

Sold by all Booksellers, Newspaper-agents, and Venders of Periodicals.

⁎ ORDER "ALFRED CARLILE'S PORTRAITS."

THE CHARTISTS!

JOHN FROST, ZEPHANIAH WILLIAMS, AND JONES THE WATCHMAKER.

ON WEDNESDAY, the 4th of FEBRUARY, was published, on a large-sized sheet of drawing paper, price Sixpence,

ACCURATE PORTRAITS

of these three condemned men, on whom the following awful sentence has been passed :—

The sentence of the law is—" *That each of you, John Frost, Zephaniah Williams, and William Jones, be taken hence to the place from whence you came, and be thence taken on a hurdle to the place of execution, and that each of you be then hung by the neck until you be dead, and that afterwards the head of each of you shall be severed from his body, and the body of each, divided into four quarters, to be disposed of as her Majesty shall think fit; and may the Lord have mercy upon your souls.*"

A considerable allowance to the trade on taking quantities.

Glover, Publisher, Water-lane, Fleet-street, London, and all country booksellers.

Why do n't you buy the " Odd Fellow ?"

Confessedly the best of all the cheap publications.   Publishing weekly, twenty columns of closely-printed matter, price One Penny, with a comic caricature by an eminent artist.

THE ODD FELLOW; a collection of every thing instructive, interesting, and humorous. Short, pithy, well-told tales; entertaining narratives; extraordinary and curious facts in science and literature ; witty sayings; sparkling poetic gems ; lively accounts of all sorts of odd fellows, and funny things of every description,   Also, original notices of the London Theatres, and of popular living actors; interesting dramatic intelligence from the best sources. &c. &c.

H. Hetherington, 126, Strand ; and all booksellers and newsmen in town and country.

LIFE OF

JACK SHEPPARD

𝕿𝖍𝖊 𝕳𝖔𝖚𝖘𝖊𝖇𝖗𝖊𝖆𝖐𝖊𝖗.

LONDON:

GLOVER, WATER LANE, FLEET STREET.

M. DCCC. XL.

List of Illustrations.

Contents.

JACK SHEPPARD IN HIS INFANCY IS NOT FRIENDLESS.

Printed by W Clerk 202 High Holborn

B.

LIFE OF JACK SHEPPARD.

CHAPTER I.

BIRTH OF JACK SHEPPARD.

On the night of the 26th of November, 1703, London was visited by a fearful storm, which, as historians inform us, "surpassed all that the oldest inhabitants recollected, or had ever heard of."

It was profoundly dark, and the wind which had began to blow with great violence, chased the clouds rapidly across the heavens, and dispersed the vapours hanging nearer the earth. Sometimes the moon was totally eclipsed; at others, it shed a wan and ghastly glimmer over the masses rolling in the firmament. Not a star could be discovered; but, in their stead, streaks of lurid radiance shot ever and anon athwart the dusky vault, and added to the ominous appearance of the night.

It was a night of storm and terror, and promised each moment to be more stormy and more terrible. The darkness was almost palpable; and the wind, which had been blowing in gusts, was the next minute suddenly lulled. Anon, a roar like a volley of ordnance, was heard aloft, and the wind again burst its bondage—the gale became a hurricane. That hurricane was the most terrible that ever laid waste a city. Destruction everywhere marked its course. Steeples toppled, and towers reeled beneath its fury. Trees were torn up by the roots, and houses were levelled with the ground—others were unroofed; the leads on the churches were stripped off, and shrivelled up like rolls of parchment. All was darkness, horror, confusion, ruin! Men fled from their tottering habitations, and returned to them scared by greater dangers. The end of the world seemed at hand.

During this fearful time, an insensible female was hurried along the dilapidated streets of the 'Mint,' in Southwark, by a noisy and turbulent rabble, who were uttering most discordant yells, and aided by cows-horns, rattles, tin cannisters filled with stones, bladders and catgut, and other instruments of what is not inappropriately styled 'rough music,' appeared vainly attempting to drown the voice of the elements. It was a party of 'Minters' returning from witnessing the execution of a malefactor at Tyburn; and were, doubtless, offering a requiem for their departed 'pal.'

The inhabitants of the Mint were a peculiar race, always on the alert to maintain their privileges, and to assist each other against the attacks of their common enemy—the sheriff's officer. It was only by the adoption of such a course, that the inviolability of the asylum could be preserved. Incursions were often made upon its territories by the functionaries of the law; sometimes attended with success, but more frequently with discomfiture; and it rarely happened, unless by stratagem or bribery, that (in the language of the gentlemen of the short staff) an important caption could be effected. In order to guard against accidents or surprises, watchmen, or scouts, (as they were styled,) were stationed at the three main outlets of the sanctuary, ready to give the signal in the manner just described: bars were erected, which, in case of emergency, could be immediately stretched across the streets; doors were attached to the alleys, and never opened without due precautions; gates were affixed to the courts, wickets to the gates, and bolts to the wickets. The back windows of the houses (where any such existed) were strongly barricaded, and kept constantly shut; and the fortress was, furthermore, defended by high walls and deep ditches, in those quarters where it appeared most exposed. There was also a Maze, (the name is still retained in the district,) into which the debtor could run; and through the intricacies of which it was impossible for an officer to follow him, without a clue. Whoever chose to incur the risk of so doing might enter the Mint at any hour; but no one was suffered to depart without giving a satisfactory account of himself, or producing a pass from 'the Master.' In short, every contrivance that ingenuity could devise, was resorted to by this horde of reprobates to secure themselves from danger or molestation.

The female already mentioned as being borne along in the midst of the mob, was the 'Hempen Widow,' the relict of the man who has expiated his crimes by death at the hangman's hands upon 'Tyburn Tree.' Her body was hurried into a dirty thoroughfare, called Wheeler's Rents, running from Mint Street through a variety of turnings into Saint George's Fields. The neighbouring houses were tenanted by the lowest order of thieves, mendicants, and other worthless and nefarious characters, who fled thither to escape the punishment due to their various crimes ; for the 'Old Mint,' although it had been divested of some of its privileges as a sanctuary, still afforded a safe asylum. Into the most wretched of these houses was the inanimate body borne ; and the door closed against all, save an old crone or two, whose services were likely to be requisite ; the wretched woman being far advanced in pregnancy, and premature labour anticipated to result from the shock her feelings had sustained in witnessing the death of the father of her unborn child. A few persons unacquainted with the particulars, made anxious inquiries of the gossips, whose curiosity kept them lingering round the door, and learnt, that the newly made widow had, with her husband, resided in the 'Mint' about five months—he having been compelled to seek shelter in its sanctuary. But, after a time, venturing boldly to pursue his 'profession' as a burglar, had been caught, tried, and condemned. His wife had paid a farewell visit on the morning of his execution, and, at his earnest request, had accompanied the cavalcade from Newgate to Tyburn ; where, on the cart being drawn from under the condemned man, she had uttered a shriek, and fallen senseless into the arms of her companions, and had been by them brought home in melancholy triumph. A hand-bill was produced, purporting to be " *The last dying speech and confession of* TOM SHEPPARD, *the notorious housebreaker, who was hung at Tyburn on the 26th of November*, 1703 : " a rude wood-cut at the top represented the wretched malefactor dangling from the 'triple tree.'

The hurricane had now reached its climax. The blast shrieked, as if exulting in its wrathful mission. Stunning and continuous, the din seemed almost to take away the power of hearing. He, who had faced the gale, would have been instantly stifled. Piercing through every crevice in the clothes, it, in some cases, tore them from the wearer's limbs, or from his grasp. It penetrated the skin ; benumbed the flesh ; paralysed the faculties. The intense darkness added to the terror of the storm. The destroying angel hurried by, shrouded in his gloomiest apparel. None saw, though all felt, his presence, and heard the thunder of his voice. Imagination, coloured by the obscurity, peopled the air with phantoms. Ten thousand steeds appeared to be trampling aloft, charged with the work of devastation. Awful shapes seemed to flit by, borne on the wings of the tempest, animating and directing its fury. The actual danger was lost sight of in these wild apprehensions; and many timorous beings were scared beyond reason's verge by the excess of their fears.

The violence of the storm made the few, who had remained near the house into which the widow had been carried, think of finding shelter, when a tremendous thunder-clap having dislodged part of a stack of chimnies, and brought them clattering into the street beneath, caused one of the attendants to rush forth in great trepidation to learn the extent of the damage; not being quite assured that the house she was in was not about to crumble into a heap of ruins. From this woman the loiterers learnt, that the widow had given birth to a boy, but was herself almost past hope, the shock being more than her weakened constitution could sustain. This intelligence was soon passed from one to another, and in a short time the street was deserted.

This boy was JACK SHEPPARD, whose "strange eventful history," the next chapter will further develope.

CHAPTER II.

JACK SHEPPARD IN HIS INFANCY IS NOT FRIENDLESS.

ABOUT a year after the occurrence of the events related in the preceding chapter, Mrs Sheppard's wretched habitation was visited by an elderly respectable looking man, in whose countenance benevolence was strongly marked. This person was Mr Wood, a carpenter, residing in Wych Street, in whose employ, Tom Sheppard had worked for many years, and who, learning the miserable condition of the widow and child of his once esteemed servant, had determined if possible to rescue them from the horrors he judged must attend a life passed in the Mint.

The room in which he found the widow, had once been occupied by a man called "Old Tom" whose devotedness to the bottle brought on premature decay, and eventually insanity, which caused him to seek the assistance of a halter, to end a life of wretchedness; which event was recorded by the following words, traced in charcoal on the dirty wall of the apartment:—"Old Tom" *hung himsel in this rum for luv of licker;*" accompanied by a graphic sketch of the unhappy suicide dangling from a beam; rotten and covered with a thick coat of dirt, the boards of the floor presented a most insecure footing, the

Published by Chas. Water Lane Fleet Street

Printed by Wm. S. Williams Pall Mall

JACK SHEPPARD

C.

bare walls were covered with grotesque designs of hierogliphic characters, executed in red chalk and charcoal ; the ceiling had in many places given way, the laths had been removed, and where any plaster remained, it was either mapped and blistered with damps, or festooned with cobwebs. On a small shelf near the foot of a bed stood some phials, a cracked bason, a jug without a handle, a tin coffee-pot, minus its spout, and a bit of looking-glass. The floor was one mass of filth. Mrs Sheppard was dressed in an old black gown, discoloured by various stains, and intended, it would seem, from the remnants of rusty crape with which it was here and there tricked out, to represent the garb of widowhood, and held in her arms a sleeping infant.

" You've but a sorry lodging here, Mrs Sheppard ?" said the benevolent carpenter ; and seating himself by the scanty fire, he explained to the widow the object of his visit, which was, that she should immediately remove from her present abode to a cottage which he would provide, and that his assistance, added to the produce of her own industry, should enable her to rear her child until he was old enough to be apprenticed, when the honest carpenter promised to have the boy bound to himself, and by teaching him a trade, enable him to enter the world with capabilities to become a better man than his father. The widow of course, received this offer with feelings of gratitude ; and a few days saw her settled in a cottage near London, surrounded by such comforts as the benevolence of Mr Wood could fancy necessary to her happiness, and the rearing of her sickly child.

CHAPTER III.

JACK SHEPPARD AN IDLE APPRENTICE.

NOTHING of importance occurred to our hero worth recording until he was bound apprentice to his worthy patron, honest Mr Wood, the carpenter ; if we except an incident which caused his mother no little alarm at the time, but like most circumstances of the kind, became either entirely effaced from her mind, or considered of so little import as to cause no permanent anxiety. The incident alluded to was this : a wandering gipsy, once approached a group of females, of whom Mrs Sheppard was one, and solicited leave to foretell their destinies, but not being likely to exhibit her talents profitably, was departing, when little Jack, who was in his mother's arms, stretched forth his tiny hands in evident glee, at beholding the party-coloured though showy dress of the wandering fortune-teller; the movement was not unnoticed by the woman, who, after a scrutinizing glance at the infant, exclaimed in a deep tone of voice, which seriously attracted all who heard it:

"That child, though now so artless, will live a chequered life, and end his days on the gallows, I know it by these marks!" and she drew attention to a black mole under little Jack's right ear, and a deep line in the form of a noose just above the middle of the left thumb.

This prediction cast a gloom on the spirits of the group for a time, but was ultimately ridiculed as a spiteful enamation of the disappointed mendicant.

At the age of twelve, Jack entered upon his apprenticeship, and already began to display traits of that daring recklessness which so vividly marked his after life. In appearance, Jack Sheppard was by no means unpleasing, his face was that of a quick intelligent looking boy, with fine hazel eyes, and a clear olive complexion. His figure was uncommonly slim, even for his age, and the looseness of his garb, made him appear thinner than he was in reality. Boys, at the time of which we write, were attired like men of their own day, or certain charity children of ours; Jack Sheppard wore a pair of black plush breeches, and a grey waistcoat, with immoderately large pockets. A coat was an article he generally dispensed with, finding it more convenient as well as agreeable to himself to pursue his avocations in his shirt-sleeves.

His stay with Mr Wood was but of short duration. The cause of their last quarrel and final separation is told in the following anecdote :—

Being left in the workshop one day with instructions to finish a trifling job, Jack fancied the idea of carving his name on a beam that crossed the apartment immediately above his head, and laying aside his tools, he mounted on some steps, and with a clasp knife roughly hacked the words

and to lighten the labour, amused himself by chanting a well known flash song of the day, called

THE NEWGATE STONE.

When Claude du Val was in Newgate thrown,
He carved his name on the dungeon stone ;
Quoth a dubsman, who gazed on the shattered wall,
" You have carved your epitaph, Claude du Val,
            With your chisel so fine, tra la !"

Du Val was hang'd, and the next who came
On the selfsame stone inscribed his name :
" Aha !" quoth the dubsman, with devilish glee,
" Tom Waters, *your* doom is the triple tree !
            With your chisel so fine, tra la ! "

Within that dungeon lay Captain Bew,
Rumbold and Whitney—a jolly crew !
All carved their names on the stone, and all
Share the fate of the brave Du Val !
            With their chisels so fine, tra la !

Full twenty highwaymen blithe and bold,
Rattled their chains in that dungeon old ;
Of all that number there 'scaped not one
Who carved his name on the Newgate Stone,
            With his chisel so fine, tra la !

Mr Wood happening to return earlier than anticipated, was about to enter the workshop, when not hearing the sound of labour issue from within, and suspecting that his apprentice was neglecting his employment, he paused for a moment to listen ; when finding all silent, he cautiously lifted the latch and crept into the room, resolved to punish Jack if his suspicions should prove correct. Near the door stood a pile of deal planks, behind which the carpenter ensconced himself in order to reconnoitre unobserved the proceedings of his idle apprentice. Our readers are already acquainted with Jack Sheppard's employment, which being completed, he descended from the steps, muttering to himself, " I've half a mind to give old Wood the slip, and turn highwayman. I like the life those jolly fellows have of it, who are nightly carousing at the Black Lion."

" And so you 'll turn highwayman, will you, you young rascal ?" exclaimed Wood, bustling forward and soundly cuffing Jack. " You 'll turn highwayman, eh ?"

" Yes, I will," replied Jack, " if you beat me in that way—I won't be struck for nothink.

"Nothing!" echoed Wood; "do you call neglecting your work and singing flash songs nothing? Zounds, you incorrigible rascal! many a master would have taken you before a magistrate and prayed for your solitary confinement in Bridewell. But I'll be more lenient, and content myself with chastising you." Saying which, the worthy carpenter proceeded to thrash Jack, who struggled violently, and at last succeeded in getting out of his master's grasp, when thrusting his hand into his breeches pocket, he drew forth a formidable clasp knife, and rapidly opening it, exclaimed, "Now I would n't advise you to lay hands on me again."

Mr Wood glanced on the hardy offender, and not liking the expression of his countenance, thought it advisable to postpone the further execution of his threats to a more favourable opportunity.

"Jack, Jack, you'll come to be hanged; be warned in time to avoid bad company. You may become a first rate workman, but you want one quality. You want industry, you want steadiness. Idleness is the key of beggary. Be warned by your father's fate. I've engaged to watch over you as a son, and I will do so as far as I'm able, but if you neglect my advice, what chance have I of benefiting you? I've made up my mind on one point—you shall either obey me or leave me—please yourself."

During this lecture, Jack coolly closed the knife and returned it to his capacious pocket, meantime looking on like one who is bent on following his own inclinations, though they may lead to his utter ruin.

An hour had not elapsed ere Jack had determined on quitting the hospitable roof of his friend the carpenter, which rash step was carried into execution the same night, and, as the sequel proves, was

Jack Sheppard's first step towards the gallows.

Printed by W. Clark. 202 High Holborn.

Published by F. Gluver. Water-Lane, Fleet St.

D.

JACK SHEPPARD'S FIRST ROBBERY.

CHAPTER IV.

THE BLACK LION.

JACK, on leaving his master's house, repaired at once to the Black Lion, and seated himself in the tap-room, which was filled with thieves, prostitutes, and other disreputable characters. At a glance one might see the deference paid by the lower grades of thieves to their more daring brethren ; the pickpocket, or "petty larceny vagabond," viewing the "cracksman," or housebreaker, as his superior, while the "roadster," or highwayman, was considered as the aristocrat of the profession. Jack was not at a loss for companions of his own age, for in one corner of the room were seated half a dozen boys with a dirty pack of cards and a pint of gin before them, who were laughing and gambling with a reckless glee, which proved them to be apt scholars in the academy of infamy in which they were studying. Jack's look and manner immediately recommended him to these youths, and room was made at their table for one who as it was remarked "looked of their own kidney." Sheppard threw some coppers on to the table, and imitating the manner of his fellows, called loudly for another supply of gin which was readily served ; the cards were again shuffled and dealt, and Jack for the first time in his life found himself "at home."

Time passed quickly on, and our hero becoming fuddled with the liquor he had drank, sleep pressed heavily on his eyes : he was however restored to consciousness by hearing a loud voice proclaim "order for a song ;" and a flashily dressed red whiskered man, whom Jack afterwards learnt was the celebrated Dick Turpin, chaunted forth the following :—

CHAPTER OF HIGHWAYMEN.

I.

OF every rascal of every kind,
The most notorious to my mind
Was the Cavalier Captain—gay JEMMY HIND ! *

Which nobody can deny.

---

* James Hind (the "Prince of Prigs,")—a Royalist Captain of some distinction, was hanged, drawn, and quartered, in 1652. Some good stories are told of him. He had the credit of robbing Cromwell, Bradshaw, and Peters. His discourse to Peters is particularly edifying.

II.

But the pleasantest coxcomb among them all
For lute, coranto, and madrigal,
Was the galliard Frenchman—CLAUDE DU VAL! *—

Which nobody can deny.

III.

But yet Tobygloak never a coach could rob,
Could lighten a pocket, or empty a fob,
With a neater hand than OLD MOB, OLD MOB †—

Which nobody can deny.

IV.

Nor did Housebreaker ever deal harder knocks
On the stubborn lid of a good strong box,
Than that prince of good fellows, TOM COX, TOM COX ! ‡—

Which nobody can deny.

V.

And blither fellow on broad highway,
Did never with oath bid traveller stay,
Than devil-may-care WILL HOLLOWAY ! §—

Which nobody can deny.

* See Du Val's life by Doctor Pope, or Leigh Hunt's brilliant sketch of him in *The Indicator.*

† We cannot say much in favour of this worthy, whose name was Thomas Simpson. The reason of his *sobriquet* does not appear. He was not particularly scrupulous as to his mode of appropriation. One of his sayings is, however, on record—he told a widow whom he robbed, "that the end of a woman's husband begins in tears—but the end of her tears is another husband"—"upon which," says his Chronicler, "the gentlewoman gave him about fifty guineas."

‡ Tom was a sprightly fellow, and carried his sprightliness to the gallows, for just before he was turned off he kicked Mr Smith, the ordinary, and the hangman out of the cart—a piece of pleasantry which created, as may be supposed, no small sensation.

§ Many agreeable stories are related of Holloway. His career, however, closed with a murder. He contrived to break out of Newgate, but returned to witness the trial of one of his associates; when, upon the attempt of a turnkey, one Richard Spurling, to seize him, Will knocked him on the head in the presence of the whole court. For this offence he suffered the extreme penalty of the law in 1712.

VI.

And in roguery nought could exceed the tricks
Of GETTINGS and GREY, and the five or six,
Who trod in the steps of bold NEDDY WICKS ! *—

Which nobody can deny.

VII.

Nor could any so handily break a lock
As SHEPPARD, † who stood on the Newgate dock,
And nicknamed the gaolers around him *"his flock !"*

Which nobody can deny.

VIII.

Nor did highwayman ever before possess,
For ease, for security, danger, distress,
Such a mare as DICK TURPIN's Black Bess, Black Bess!

Which nobody can deny.

Loud cheers followed this performance : the mention of the hardihood of Tom Sheppard, caused a smile to pass over the features of Jack, which proved him to be a son in every way worthy of such a father.

It was now midnight and the company began to depart, not however, before Jack,—who, during the evening, has recounted to his new companions the cause of his appearance amongst them, his anxiety to join in their exploits, and his willingness to put some of the older hands up to the secret of breaking into Mr Wood's house, at what he considered the most vulnerable part, and to show where the plate and valuables were deposited,—was welcomed as "a trump" in every way entitled to their patronage and fostering care.

Finding himself at length left alone in the room, and wishing to shake off the stupifying effects of the gin he had drank, Jack left the Black Lion, and singing snatches of the flash songs of the day, sauntered forth without any particular object in view beyond passing away the night.

Jack had been walking the streets about half an hour, when a drizzling rain began to fall, compelling him to seek shelter in the large door-way of a mansion he was passing ; and as he crouched himself into the corner, he was not

---

* Wick's adventures with Madame Toly are highly diverting. It was this hero, not Turpin, as has been erroneously stated, who stopped the celebrated Lord Mohun. Of Gettings and Grey and " the five or six," the less said the better.

† Tom Sheppard, the father of our hero.

free from some compunctious feelings, arising from the contrast his situation then afforded, to the comfortable bed he had occupied the previous night in the carpenter's house. Jack was, however, not in a condition to meditate, and his stupified senses were soon locked in a sound sleep.

CHAPTER V.

JACK SHEPPARD'S FIRST ROBBERY.

'T WAS seven o'clock ere Jack awoke in the morning; and, from sleeping in the open air without covering of any kind, he felt his limbs so stiffened and benumbed, that it was with difficulty he managed to stand upon his legs. Sincerely did he repent the rashness of the step he had taken, but pride would not allow him to think of returning to Mr Wood to crave forgiveness; and after spending a quarter of an hour of the bitterest reflection, he determined on visiting his mother; instinctively feeling, that in a mother's arms a child may always find a sanctuary, be he ever so stained with sin.

Acting upon this determination, Jack made an effort to quit himself of the sensation of benumbedness which pervaded his frame: and with painful steps commenced his journey towards Willesden, a secluded village in the neighbourhood of the metropolis.

In passing through the Old Bailey, his progress was arrested by the sight of Newgate: and, as evidence of the hardened disposition of the boy, his spirits seemed to revive, as with an eager curiosity he scanned the sombre-looking and massive walls of the prison: he instantly appeared in another character—the thoughts of those who were confined within the building he gazed upon, seeming to raise afresh his incipient desire for a similar life to theirs; and after a short pause he pursued his errand with a lighter and quicker step.

About an hour's walking brought Jack within sight of Willesden — a charming spot,—with its scattered farm-houses and noble granges, and its old grey church tower just appearing above a grove of rook-haunted trees.

Our hero soon came near to his mother's abode—a little cottage standing

Published by P. Glover, Water Lane, Fleet St

F.

JACK SHEPPARD'S FIRST ESCAPE.

Printed by W Clerk 202 High Holborn

in the outskirts of the village—but paused ere he approached. Not perceiving anything which betokened animation, he concluded his mother was away from home; and the sound of the church bells at once reminded him, that (it being Sunday) his parent had repaired to the house of God, in which she had latterly sincerely addressed herself to her Maker with fervent devotion.

Jack Sheppard approached the cottage, and finding the door fastened, he made an entry through the window; and after satisfying his appetite with the contents of an old fashioned cupboard, which, thanks to the generosity of Mr Wood! the widow never kept very bare, he threw himself on his mother's bed, and soon fell asleep.

After an hour's slumber in the peaceful cottage of his parent, Jack Sheppard awoke; and being much refreshed, he sauntered out towards the church, in the expectation of meeting his mother. He reached the church door, and sat himself down on an oaken bench in the porch, intending to await the departure of the congregation. At this moment, a gentleman clad in a scarlet hunting coat, and the etceteras of a fashionable riding suit, entered the porch, and pausing ere he proceeded into the church, drew from his pocket a massive golden snuff box; and having satisfied his olfactory nerves with a pinch of the titillating powder, returned it to his pocket, and passed on. This movement had not been unobserved by Jack, whose fingers instinctively itched to possess such a treasure; and he involuntarily followed the gentleman into the church.

The pews were all full, and the owner of the box our hero coveted, seemed by no means disconcerted at the necessity there was for his taking his station at the side of the pews in the middle aisle, which afforded him an opportunity of displaying his figure to the greatest advantage.

Jack stealthily followed the gentleman, and seated himself on the end of one of the free seats which were arranged in the aisle; his eye intently fixed on the pocket into which he had seen the snuff-box returned. Jack in his abstraction had not observed that the position he occupied in the church, was but two seats before that on which his mother was sitting. The widow, who was engaged in prayer when the gentleman, followed by the boy, entered the church, but partly suppressed an expression of astonishment on beholding her son.

Jack could not withstand the temptation thus thrown in his way; and, adroitly gliding his hand into the pocket of the riding coat, drew forth the box. The movement had, however, been observed by his mother; and when the horrid truth flashed across her brain,—that even in the sacred edifice appropriated to the worship of HIM, who has said, "*Thou shalt not steal!*" her boy had become a thief, she uttered a loud scream, and fell swooning on the floor of the church.

All eyes were instantly attracted to the spot where the widow was lying, and the stranger turning suddenly, perceived his box in the hand of the young culprit; he was about to grasp Jack, but like an eel he slipped from beneath the extended hand, and with the utmost swiftness darted out of the church; but he was not lost sight of, and an immediate pursuit took place.

Amidst the shouts of twenty voices exclaiming " stop thief! stop thief!" Jack bounded over the tomb stones, and with a celerity almost inconceivable, leapt over the church-yard wall into the road.

Jack was a good runner and put his speed to the test; but a circumstance occurred which was quite unforeseen, and rendered his speed of little avail. A horseman happened to be passing a moment after the outcry was made in issuing from the church, and hastily gathering the particulars, he clapped spurs to his horse, and joined or rather headed the pursuers.

Against such odds Jack could not of course stand a chance, and slackening his pace, soon found himself in the grasp of his mounted pursuer, who, throwing himself from his horse, seized the thief by the collar, and turned to meet the mob of the congregation, who had quitted the sacred edifice in consternation.

A fainting woman was borne along from the church by a number of females,—it was Mrs Sheppard; and as Jack gazed on her pallid features and motionless frame, his heart smote him, and he turned from the distressing spectacle.

On the road they met the beadle, into whose custody Jack was delivered; and after glancing hastily round in search of any face he could recognise, and finding none, he rallied from the shock his feelings had sustained on beholding his mother, and commenced humming the burden of a flash song.

After a brief consultation amongst the authorities, it was decided that the culprit should be confined in the cage of Willesden parish, until the following morning.

CHAPTER VI.

JACK SHEPPARD'S FIRST ESCAPE.

WILLESDEN cage in which Jack Sheppard was confined, was a small building about eight feet high, with a number of boards affixed to it, inscribed with sundry admonitory notices to gipsies and other vagrants, and guide posts to direct the wayfarer. The cage had a strong door with an iron grating at the top, which was securely fastened by a large padlock. A number of patchings might have been observed, remedying the ravages of time on the old-fashioned building.

For some time after the young thief had been secured as has been described, he remained in a very dejected state—he had not foreseen such a result as he experienced on his first attempt at robbery, he did not know what might become of him; and the sad spectacle his mother presented, preyed heavily upon his mind, which was not naturally so callous as to be wholly insensible to the stings of conscience; tears involuntarily fell from his eyes, and at length wearied with thinking on the past, and terrified at the prospect of the future, he composed himself to sleep.

It was evening, ere Jack awoke; and shivering with cold and hunger, he felt his condition truly wretched. At length the door of the cage was unlocked, and the beadle presented himself with a pitcher of water and a small loaf; and after glancing carefully round to convince himself that all was right, the parochial functionary cautioned his prisoner to be careful of the provision, as he would get nothing more till the morning.

"Very well, old cock'd-hat," said Jack, swigging heartily at the water; "I'll take care —but could n't you let us have a drop of gin? this water is devilish cold stuff."

The horrified look of the beadle as he withdrew himself from the cage, caused Jack no little merriment, and he seemed at once to banish all compunctious feelings, and began steadily to contemplate his chances of escape; the door was too strong, the walls too thick: the ceiling, if he could reach it, presented the most likely outlet. After satisfying his hunger, Jack determined to attempt a breach in the roof, but hearing the tramp of passengers on the road, he thought it better to postpone the commencement of his labours until a later hour of the night.

Willesden church clock struck eleven, as Jack began to climb towards the roof of his prison, in which step he was aided by certain inequalities in the door. He soon began to pick away a quantity of the plaster, and breaking off several laths, he contrived, but not without some difficulty, to force up one of the tiles; the worst of the labour was now over, and he made an aperture large enough to allow his body to pass through, and by the aid of the sign post dragged himself unto the roof.

Thus did Jack Sheppard effect his first escape.

CHAPTER VII.

JACK'S FIRST INTERVIEW WITH JONATHAN WILD.

JACK sat himself down on the roof of the cage to rest himself, and free his eyes and mouth from the dust, with which his late exertions had covered him; he had not waited many seconds before he heard the sound of horses approaching, and glancing along the road, he perceived two men riding at a rapid pace towards the cage. Jack immediately crouched behind the large boards on the roof, intending to remain unobserved until the horsemen had passed.

They approached, and to Jack's horror pulled up in front of the cage, when one of them dismounted and approached the door; Jack at once concluded they were officers of justice sent to convey him to a stronger place of confinement, and his heart sunk within him, as he heard the clinking of what appeared to him to be the keys of his *late* prison. He scarcely breathed as he heard the man applying himself to the padlock and muttering. At length, the mounted man exclaimed—

"Quick! quick! or we shall be observed, and have our trouble only for our pains; surely Bill, thou art not such a bungler at picking a lock?"

The man thus addressed uttered a volley of oaths, and made more desperate exertions to force the fastening; while Jack was thinking of dropping from the roof and secreting himself behind the cage, being at a loss to conjecture the nature of the visit these strangers had paid his place of confinement.

Published by J. Glover Water Lane Fleet St.

F.

JACK SHEPPARD GETS DRUNK.

Printed by W. Clerk 202 High Holborn.

" After all," said one of the men, " the young rascal may not be worth the trouble we are taking, but we 'll not turn back now ;" and with a sharp movement of the wire he was using he succeeded in throwing back the bolt of the padlock; " there it is," he continued, as he removed the fastnings of the door, and attempted to push it open, " now, my gallows'-bird, you 'er at liberty." The rubbish which had fallen from the roof during Jack's labor impeded the opening of the door, without a little force being used ; when the man entered the cage, and at once perceived the hole in the ceiling, exclaimed, " by God, the bird has flown ! we are done now, any how ; and producing a dark lantern from his pocket, he proceeded to examine the place. At length, happening to cast the strong rays of light which streamed from the lantorn towards the roof, he discovered the fugitive, who was about to lower himself on the outside.

" Ha ! ha ! my boy, you 're there, are you ?" roared the man as he darted out, and caught Jack just as he reached the ground.

" Why, what the devil 's this ?" exclaimed he who had kept his saddle ; " have you broken out of the cage, Jack ?"

" It do n't look unlike it," replied the boy ; it must be a stronger prison than Willesden cage that can hold me."

" Bravo !" exclaimed one of his new companions, " that beats all I ever heard of ; but lose no time, jump up behind me, you 're safe now ; a short gallop, and we shall be beyond the reach of your enemies ; give him a leg up, Bill, and let 's be off."

Jack was hoisted on to the horse by the fellow that had picked the lock ; who, after gathering up his tools, vaulted on to his saddle and followed his companion ; who, with Jack's arms riveted round his waist, had galloped off at a rapid pace towards London.

During their ride, Jack Sheppard learnt that his companion was the notorious Jonathan Wild, the thieftaker, who explained his motive for attempting to release Jack, as arising from a favorable impression, the report of his theft in Willesden church had made in his mind, and who promised Jack that if he would place himself under his tuition, that he should become one of the finest thieves of the day, which so entirely agreed with the boy's fancy, that he readily consented to the proposition.

As the thieftaker will be conspicuously associated with our hero throughout this memoir, we cannot resist giving a description of him in the language of a modern writer, who, in the spirit of romance, has depicted many of the most celebrated characters of by gone days.

Jonathan Wild, at this time, was on the high-road to the greatness which he subsequently, and not long afterwards, obtained. He was fast rising to an eminence that no one of his nefarious profession ever reached before him, nor, it is to be hoped, will ever reach again. He was the Napoleon of knavery, and established an uncontrolled empire over all the practitioners of crime. This was no light conquest; nor was it a government easily maintained. Resolution, severity, subtlety, were required for it; and these were qualities which Jonathan possessed in an extraordinary degree. The danger or difficulty of an exploit never appalled him. What his head conceived his hand executed. Professing to stand between the robber and the robbed, he himself plundered both. He it was who formed the grand design of a robber corporation, of which he should be the sole head and director, with the right of delivering those who concealed their booty, or refused to share it with him, to the gallows. He divided London into districts; appointed a gang to each district; and a leader to each gang, whom he held responsible to himself. The country was partitioned in a similar manner. Those whom he retained about his person, or placed in offices of trust, were for the most part convicted felons, who, having returned from transportation before their term had expired, constituted, in his opinion, the safest agents, inasmuch as they could neither be legal evidences against him, nor withhold any portion of the spoil of which he chose to deprive them. But the crowning glory of Jonathan, that which raised him above all his predecessors in iniquity, and clothed his name with undying notoriety—was when in the plenitude of his power, he commenced a terrible trade, till then unknown—namely, a traffic in human blood. This he carried on by procuring witnesses to swear away the lives of those persons who had incurred his displeasure, or whom it might be necessary to remove.

Jack's audacious manner now that he found himself on what he thought the high road to preferment, evidently pleased Jonathan Wild, who at once perceived that he could find in Sheppard a valuable auxiliary in his nefarious practices; Jonathan had observed Jack's conduct on the previous night at the Black Lion, and saw at once that the boy possessed all the elements of roguery in great perfection.

They now approached Jonathan Wild's residence in the Old Bailey; it was a large dismal-looking habitation, separated from the street by a flagged court-yard, and defended from general approach by an iron railing. Even in the daylight, it had a sombre and suspicious air, and seemed to slink back from the adjoining houses, as if afraid of their society. In the dim light of breaking morning, in which it was now seen, it looked like a prison, and, indeed, it was Jonathan's fancy to make it resemble one as much as possible. The windows were grated, the doors barred; each room had the name as well as the appearance of a cell; and the very porter who stood at the gate, habited like a gaoler, with his huge bunch of keys at his girdle, his forbidding countenance and surly demeanor seemed to be borrowed from Newgate. The clanking of chains, the grating of locks, and the rumbling of bolts must have been music in Jonathan's ears, so much pains did he take to subject himself to such sounds. The scanty furniture of the rooms corresponded with their dungeon-like aspect. The walls were bare, and painted in stone-color; the floors, devoid of carpet; the beds, of hangings; the windows, of blinds; and, excepting in the thieftaker's own audience-chamber, there was not a chair or a table about the premises; the place of these conveniences being elsewhere supplied by benches, and deal-boards laid across joint-stools. Great stone staircases leading no one knew whither, and long gloomy passages, impressed the occasional visitor with the idea that he was traversing a building of vast extent; and, though this was not the case in reality, the deception was so cleverly contrived that it seldom failed of producing the intended effect. Scarcely any one entered Mr Wild's dwelling without apprehension, or quitted it without satisfaction. More strange stories were told of it than of any other house in London. The garrets were said to be tenanted by coiners, and artists employed in altering watches and jewelry; the cellars to be used as a magazine for stolen goods. By some it was affirmed that a subterranean communication existed between the thief-taker's abode and Newgate, by means of which he was enabled to maintain a secret correspondence with the imprisoned felons: by others, that an underground passage led to extensive vaults, where such malefactors as he chose to screen from justice might lie concealed till the danger was blown over. Nothing, in short, was too extravagant to be related of it; and Jonathan, who delighted in investing himself and his residence with mystery, encouraged, and perhaps originated, these marvellous tales. However this may be, such was the ill report of the place that few passed along the Old Bailey without bestowing a glance of fearful curiosity at its dingy walls, and wondering what was going on inside them; while fewer still, of those who paused at the door, read without some internal trepidation, the formidable name—inscribed in large letters on its brass-plate—of JONATHAN WILD.

Arrived at his habitation, Jonathan knocked in a peculiar manner at the door, which was instantly opened by the grim-visaged porter just alluded to. No sooner had they crossed the threshold than a fierce barking was heard at the farther extremity of the passage, and, at the next moment, a couple of mastiffs of the largest size rushed furiously towards them. Jack Sheppard stood upon his defence; but he would unquestionably have been torn in pieces by the savage hounds, if a shower of oaths, seconded by a vigorous application of kicks and blows from their master, had not driven them growling off. As-

cending the stairs, and conducting them along a sombre gallery, in which
Jack noticed that every door was painted black, and numbered, he stopped at
the entrance of a chamber ; and, selecting a key from the bunch at his girdle,
unlocked it.   Following his guide, Sheppard found himself in a large and lofty
apartment, the extent of which he could not entirely discern until lights were
set upon the table.   He then looked around him with some curiosity ; and, as
the thieftaker was occupied in giving directions to his attendant in an under-
tone, ample leisure was allowed him for investigation.   At the first glance,
he imagined he must have stumbled upon a museum of rarities, there were so
many glass cases, so many open cabinets, ranged against the walls ; but the
next convinced him that if Jonathan was a virtuoso, his tastes did not run in
the ordinary channels.   Jack was tempted to examine the contents of some of
these cases.   In one was gathered together a vast assortment of weapons, each
of which, as appeared from the ticket attached to it, had been used as an in-
strument of destruction.   On this side was a razor with which a son had mur-
dered his father ; the blade notched, the haft crusted with blood : on that, a
bar of iron, bent, and partly broken, with which a husband had beaten out his
wife's brains.   As it is not, however, our intention to furnish a complete cata-
logue of these curiosities, we shall merely mention that in front of them lay a
large and sharp knife, once the property of the public executioner, and used
by him to dissever the limbs of those condemned to death for high-treason ;
together with an immense two-pronged flesh-fork, likewise employed by the
same terrible functionary to plunge the quarters of his victims in the cauldrons
of boiling tar and oil.   Such was the room in which Jonathan Wild welcomed
Jack Sheppard, with an assurance that he was safe under his roof, until the
robbery at Willesden church and his first escape was blown over.

JACK SHEPPARD, A HOUSEBREAKER.

G.

Published by J. Clover, Water Lane, Fleet St.

Printed by W Clerk, 20 High Holborn

CHAPTER VIII.

JACK'S FUTURE LIFE DECIDED.

JACK Sheppard lay concealed for some weeks, and only ventured to leave his hiding place when the darkness of the night allowed him to roam unobserved. Not that he was likely to be recognised, although the robbery of Willesden Church and daring escape of the young thief had created a considerable sensation among the lovers of the marvellous.

Jonathan Wild in due time commenced the execution of the plans he had arranged for Jack's future life, and the first step was to make him acquainted with all the vice and infamy London contained. With this intent Jack was introduced to the frequenters of the lowest pot houses, and soon proved himself capable of realising the most sanguine expectations of his tutor.

*   *   *   *   *   *

A year or two passed away, and Jack Sheppard appeared the most perfect specimen of a thief the fancy can imagine. He had been engaged in numerous exploits of a nefarious character, in which he acquitted himself with such extraordinary skill that his name already began to be mentioned by his ‘pals’ with admiration and delight.

About this time he became acquainted with a girl, who, as she will figure conspicuously in the future pages of this memoir, shall be formally introduced to the reader.

Edgeworth Bess (so called from the town in Middlesex where she was born) was not more than seventeen, though her person had all the maturity of twenty. She had delicate oval features, light laughing blue eyes, teeth of pearly whiteness, and a brilliant complexion set off by rich auburn hair, and a very white neck and shoulders.

Although possessed of such attractions, Bess was of a depraved and wicked disposition, and the influence she had upon the actions of Jack tended to tighten the bonds which united him to a life of infamy.

Fascinated with the beauty of this girl, Jack Sheppard deemed himself the happiest of mortals when he discovered a return of his passion on the part of Bess; and not caring much for the decorum used in general society, they soon lived together as man and wife.

CHAPTER IX.

THE FLASH KEN.

Mrs Sheppard had not seen her son for many months, nor knew she where he was. Numerous reports had reached her of his many depredations, and the widow was nearly broken hearted. Having made an enquiry of one of the inhabitants of the mint, who in her husband's life-time she had been acquainted with, she learnt that on a certain night Jack was engaged to spend the evening at a noted flash ken in the Mint. She determined on seeing her boy and attempting by persuasion to turn him from the horrid course he was pursuing. With this intent she proceeded to the Mint on the night appointed.

In an incredible short space of time,—for her anxiety lent wings to her feet,—Mrs. Sheppard reached the debtors' garrison. From a scout stationed at the northern entrance, whom she addressed in the jargon of the place, with which long usage had formerly rendered her familiar, she ascertained that a youth, whom she knew by the description must be her son. had arrived there about three hours before, and had proceeded to the Cross Shovels. This was enough for the poor widow. She felt she was now near her boy, and, nothing doubting her ability to rescue him from his perilous situation, she breathed a fervent prayer for his deliverance; and, bending her steps toward the tavern in question, revolved within her mind as she walked along the best means of accomplishing her purpose. Aware of the cunning and desperate characters of the persons with whom she would have to deal,—aware, also, that she was in a quarter where no laws could be appealed to, nor assistance obtained, she felt the absolute necessity of caution. Accordingly when she arrived at the Shovels, with which, as an old haunt in by gone days of wretchedness she was well acquainted, instead of entering the principle apartment, which she saw at a glance was crowded with company of both sexes, she turned into a small room on the left of the bar, and, as an excuse for so doing, called for something to drink. The drawers at the moment were too busy to attend to her, and she seized the opportunity of examining, unperceived, the assemblage within, through a little curtained window that overlooked the adjoining chamber. The Master of the Mint, in the exercise of his two-fold office of govenor and publican, was mounted upon a chair, and holding forth to his guests in a speech, to which Mrs. Sheppard was unwillingly compelled to listen.

"Gentlemen of the Mint," said the orator, I have a toast to propose, which I am sure will be received, as it deserves to be, with enthusiasm. It is the health of a stranger,—of Mr. John Sheppard. His father was one of my old customers, and I am happy to find his son treading in his steps. He could n't be in better hands than those in which he has placed himself. Gentlemen,— Mr. Sheppard's good health, and success to him!"

The toast was received with loud applause, and he sat down amid the cheers of the company, and a universal clatter of mugs and glasses ; the widow's eye wandered quickly over the riotous and disorderly assemblage, until it settled upon one group more riotous and disorderly than the rest, of which her son formed the principle figure. The agonised mother could scarcely repress a scream at the spectacle that met her gaze. There sat Jack, evidently in the last stage of intoxication, with his collar opened, his dress disarranged, a pipe in his mouth, a bowl of punch and a half emptied rummer before him,—there he sat, receiving and returning, or rather attempting to return,—for he was almost past consciousness,—the blandishments of a female, who had passed her arm round his neck, and appeared from her gestures to be whispering soft nonsense into his ear.

On an empty cask, which served him for a chair, and opposite Jack Sheppard, whose rapid progress in depravity afforded him the highest satisfaction, sat Jonathan Wild encouraging the woman in her odious task, and plying his victim with the glass as often as he deemed it expedient to do so. By this time, he had apparently accomplished all he desired; for moving the liquor out of Jack's reach, he appropriated it entirely to his own use. One object alone, we have said, riveted Mrs Sheppard's attention ; and no sooner did she in some degree recover from the shock occasioned by the sight of her son's debased condition, than, regardless of any other consideration except his instant removal from the contaminating society by which he was surrounded, and utterly forgetting the more cautious plan she meant to have adopted, she rushed into the room, and summoned him to follow her.

"Halloa!" cried Jack, looking round, and trying to fix his inebriate gaze upon the speaker,—"who 's that ?"

" Your mother," replied Mrs Sheppard. " Come home directly, sir."

" Mother be ——!" returned Jack. " Who is it, Bess ?"

" How should I know ?" replied Edgeworth Bess. " But if it is your mother, send her about her business."

" That I will," replied Jack, in the twinkling of a bed-post."

" Glad to see you once more in the Mint, Mrs Sheppard," roared Wild, who anticipated some fun. " Come and sit down by me."

"Take a glass of gin, ma'am," cried a woman, holding up a bottle of spirit; "it used to be your favourite liquor, I 've heard."

"Jack, my love," cried Mrs Sheppard, disregarding the taunt, "come away."

"Not I," replied Jack; "I 'm too comfortable where I am.   Be off!"

"Jack!" exclaimed his unhappy parent.

"Mr Sheppard, if you please ma'am," interrupted the lad; "I allow nobody to call me Jack.   Do I, Bess, eh?"

"Nobody whatever, love," replied Edgeworth Bess; "nobody but me, dear."

"Jack," cried his mother, wringing her hands in distraction, "you 'll break my heart!"

"Poh! poh!" returned her son; "women do n't so easily break their hearts. Do they, Bess?"

"Certainly not," replied the young lady appealed to, "especially about their sons."

"Wretch!" cried Mrs Sheppard, bitterly.

"I say," retorted Edgeworth Bess, with a very unfeminine imprecation, "I shan't stand any more of that nonsense.   What do you mean by calling me wretch, madam?" she added, marching up to Mrs Sheppard, and regarding her with an insolent and threatening glance.

"Yes—what do you mean, ma'am?" added Jack, staggering after her.

"Come with me, my love, come – come," cried his mother, seizing his hand, and endeavoring to force him away.

"He shan't go," cried Edgeworth Bess, holding him by the other hand.

"I'm my own master now," cried Jack, "and I 'll do as I please.   I 'll turn cracksman, like my father—rob old Wood—he has chests full of money, and I know where they 're kept—I 'll rob him, and give the swag to you, Bess— I 'll—"

He would have said more; but, losing his balance, he fell to the ground, and, when taken up, was perfectly insensible.   In this state, he was laid upon a bench, to sleep off his drunken fit, while his wretched mother, in spite of her passionate supplications and resistance, was, by Wild's command, forcibly ejected from the house, and driven out of the Mint.

Published by E.Grover, Water Lane, Fleet St.

W.Clerk Lith. 112.High Holborn

H.

JACK QUARRELS WITH JONATHAN WILD.

CHAPTER X.

THE BURGLARY.—THE MURDER.

OUR hero, it will be seen, is on the high road to Tyburn; and neither the voice of his mother, nor the execrations of all good men could cause him to swerve from the path he seemed doomed to tread. In appearance he was much changed; the dissipated and profligate life he had led of late tending to harden his features, and gave him a peculiar scampish air. He had grown much taller, and appeared more robustly formed than in his younger days—cunning and knavery were strongly imprinted in his physiognomy: his complexion was that of a gipsy, his nose was broad and flat, and his close black crop of hair imparted a peculiar bullet-shape to his head.

Jonathan Wild had employed Sheppard in such schemes of roguery, as would mature and bring out the prime traits in his disposition; and he had so well played his part, that he was considered capable of assuming the command of any daring enterprise their nefarious calling placed in their way.

Jonathan had received information of a rich booty, which a little daring and activity might place within his grasp: a wealthy merchant had a mansion a short distance from town, and it was reported that immense hoards of plate, jewels, and money were there deposited. Wild immediately determined on securing this treasure, and entrusted Jack Sheppard with the execution of his plan.

On a fine clear night, Jack, together with a companion, started from Wild's house in the Old Bailey, and took the road towards the merchant's residence, armed with all the implements necessary to perpetrate the burglary they had in view.

It was a night well-fitted to their enterprise, calm, still, and profoundly dark. As they passed beneath the thick trees that shaded the road, the gloom was almost impenetrable. The robbers proceeded singly, and kept on the grass, so that no noise was made by their horses' feet.

As they neared the house, Jack Sheppard, who led the way, halted, and addressed his companion in a low voice:—

" I don't half like this job, I've no heart for it. Shall we turn back ?"

" And disappoint Mr Wild, captain?" remonstrated the other, in a deferential tone. "You know this is a pet project. It might be dangerous to thwart him."

"Pish!" cried Jack: "I don't value his anger a straw. All our fraternity are afraid of him; but *I* laugh at his threats. He daren't quarrel with me: and if he does, let him look to himself. I've reasons for disliking this job."

"Well, you know I act under your orders, captain, and if you give the word to retreat, I shall obey, of course: but I know what Edgeworth Bess will say when we go home empty-handed."

"Why, what will she say?" inquired Sheppard.

"That we were afraid," replied the other; "but never mind her."

"Ay; but I do mind her," cried Jack, upon whom his comrade's observation had produced the desired effect. "We'll do it."

"That's right, captain," rejoined his companion. "You pledged yourself to Mr Wild——"

"I did; and I never yet broke an engagement. Though a thief, Jack Sheppard is a man of his word."

"To be sure he is," acquiesced the other. "I should like to meet the man who would dare to gainsay it."

With this, they dismounted; and fastening their horses to a tree, proceeded towards the house. It was still so dark, that nothing could be distinguished except the heavy masses of timber by which the premises were surrounded; but as they advanced, lights were visible in some of the windows. Presently they came to a wall, on the other side of which the dog began to bark violently; but Sheppard tossed him a piece of prepared meat, and uttering a low growl, he became silent. They then clambered over a hedge, and scaling another wall, got into the garden at the back of the house. Treading with noiseless step over the soft mould, they soon reached the building. Arrived there, Jack felt about for a particular window; and having discovered the object of his search, and received the necessary implements from his companion, he instantly commenced operations. In a few seconds, the shutter flew open,—then the window,—and they were in the room. Jack now carefully closed the shutters, and struck a light, with which he set fire to a candle. The room they were in was a sort of closet, with the door locked outside; but this was only a moment's obstacle to Jack, who with a chisel forced back the bolt. The operation was effected with so much rapidity and so little noise, that even if any one had been on the alert, he could scarcely have detected it. They then took off their boots, and crept stealthily up stairs, treading upon the point of their toes so cautiously, that not a board creaked beneath their weight. Pausing at each door on the landing, Jack placed his ear to the key-hole, and listened intently.

He then tried the door of the merchant's bedchamber—it was locked, with the key left in it. This occasioned a little delay; but Jack, whose skill as a workman in the particular line he had chosen was unequalled, and who laughed at difficulties, speedily cut out a panel by means of a centre-bit and knife, took the key from the other side, and unlocked the door. Covering his face with a crape mask, and taking the candle from his associate, Jack entered the room; and, pistol in hand, stepped up to the bed, and approached the light to the eyes of the sleeper. The loud noise proceeding from the couch proved that his slumbers were deep and real; and unconscious of the danger he stood in, the old gentleman turned over to obtain a more comfortable position. During this movement, Jack grasped his pistol, held in his breath, and motioned to his companion, who bared a long knife. The momentary alarm over, he threw a piece of wash leather over a bureau, so as to deaden the sound, and instantly broke it open with a small crow-bar. While Jack was filling his pockets with golden coin from this store, the other had pulled the plate-chest from under the bed, and having forced it open, began filling a canvass bag with its contents,—silver coffee-pots, chocolate-dishes, waiters, trays, tankards, goblets, and candlesticks. It might be supposed that these articles, when thrust together into the bag, would have jingled; but these skilful practitioners managed matters so well that no noise was made. After rifling the room of everything portable, including some ornaments and wearing apparel, they prepared to depart. Jack, however, intimated his intention of visiting the other chambers, in which several articles of value were known to be kept; but the merchant, whose slumbers had been disturbed, opened his eyes and beheld the housebreakers in his apartment;—he darted suddenly from the bed and seized Jack Sheppard.

The light was instantly extinguished. But Jack found it impossible to make off,—at least with the spoil, — the old man having laid hold of the canvass-bag.

"Give back the things!" cried he. "Help, help!"

"Leave go! thundered Sheppard—"leave go—you'd better!"—and he held the sack as firmly as he could with one hand, while with the other he searched for his knife.

"No, I won't leave go!" screamed his assailant. "Fire!—murder!—thieves!—I've got one of 'em!"

"Come along," cried Jack's companion.

"I can't," answered he. "This devil has got hold of the sack. Leave go, I tell you!" and he forced open the knife with his teeth.

"Help!—murder!—thieves!—help!"

"Coming!" cried a voice from another room. "Where are you?"

" Here," replied the old gentleman. " Help—I 'll hold him !"

" Leave him," cried Jack's assistant ; darting down stairs amid a furious ringing of bells,—" the house is alarmed,—follow me !"

" Curses light on you !" exclaimed Sheppard savagely ; " since you won't be advised, take your fate."

And seizing him by the hair, he pulled back his head and drew the knife with all his force across the old man's throat. There was a dreadful stifled groan, and he fell heavily upon the landing.

The screams of the unfortunate old man had aroused the servants from their slumbers. They heard the struggle on the landing, the fall of the heavy body, the groan,—and excited almost to fienzy by fear, succeeded in forcing open the door. By this time, several of the domestics appeared with lights. A terrible spectacle was presented to their gaze : — the floor deluged with blood— and before them, the mangled and lifeless body of their master. At this juncture, a cry was raised by a servant from below, that the robbers were flying through the garden. Darting to a window looking in that direction, the butler threw it up, and discharged both his pistols, but without effect. In another minute, the tramp of horses' feet told that the perpetrators of the outrage had effected their escape.

CHAPTER XI.

JACK SHEPPARD QUARRELS WITH JONATHAN WILD.

THE frightful incident detailed in the preceding chapter, caused an immense sensation, and large rewards were offered for the discovery of the perpetrators of the murder : Jack and his companion succeeded in reaching Jonathan Wild's house safely, and there lay concealed for some time; and so well had their plans been matured and executed, that it is presumed, the mystery which veiled this horrible event would not have been cleared up, but for the circumstance of a quarrel between Sheppard and Wild, the particulars of which, were these :—

Jack Sheppard and Edgeworth Bess had for some time occupied apartments in an obscure thoroughfare in St Giles's ; and during Jack's temporary hide in the Old Bailey, Bess had lived a solitary life at the lodgings.

Jonathan Wild was occasionally commissioned with a message from Jack to

Printed by W.Clerk 202 High Holborn.

JACK AND EDGEWORTH BESS

Escaping from Clerkenwell New Prison.

I.

Published by F. Glover, Water-Lane, Fleet St.

his *ladye-love;* and it would not have been remarkable, if her charms had attracted a man of ordinary disposition and temperament; but that a man of Wild's character—a man whole body and soul seemed devoted to an endless warfare with his fellow-men, whose nature possessed not one good quality or kind feeling, should have been ensnared by the bright eyes of a pretty woman, is passing strange. Yet so it was; although we would rather think that carnal passion and not love prompted his desires.

Two months had now elapsed since the murder of the merchant; and Sheppard began to feel the estrangement from his old haunts so irksome, that he determined to brave all risks, and venture forth from his hiding place; his first visit was to Edgeworth Bess, to whose lodging we now transport the reader.

Bess was alone in her apartment, and, for one of her dissolute habits, presented an appearance of neatness and comfort, that much improved her many charms. The room she occupied, was adorned with various models of gibbets, stocks, whipping-posts, &c.—a shelf was crowded with several of these specimens of the productions of Jack Sheppard's leisure hours: amongst the most conspicuous, was a model of Newgate; another, of the pillory at Fleet Bridge; and a third, the permanent gibbet of Tyburn. On the walls of the room, were stuck several songs: such as the "*Life and Death of the Darkman's Badge;*" "*The Thief Catcher's Prophecy;*" and "*The Game of High Toby;*" which latter we shall introduce, as a sample of the flash songs a century ago:—

THE GAME OF HIGH TOBY.

I.

Now Oliver (*a*) put his black nightcap on,
    And every star its glim (*b*) is hiding,
And forth to the heath is the Scampsman (*c*) gone,
    His matchless cherry-black (*d*) prancer riding;
Merrily over the common he flies,
    Fast and free as the rush of rocket,
His crape-covered vizard drawn over his eyes,
    His tol (*e*) by his side, and his pops (*f*) in his pocket.

CHORUS.
Then who can name,
So merry a game,
As the game of all games—High Toby (g)?

II.

The traveller hears him, away! away!
    Over the wide heath he scurries;
He heeds not the thunderbolt summons to stay,
    But ever the faster and faster he hurries.

(*a*) The Moon. (*b*) Light. (*c*) Highwayman. (*d*) Cherry-colored—black; there being black cherries as well as red.—GROSE. (*e*) Sword. (*f*) Pistols. (*g*) Highway robbery.

But what daisy-cutter can match that black tit?
    He is caught—he must " stand and deliver;"
Then out with the dummy (*h*), and off with the bit (*i.*),
    Oh! the game of High Toby for ever!

CHORUS.

Then who can name
So merry a game,
As the game of all games—High Toby ?

III.

Believe me there is not a game, my brave boys,
    To compare with the game of High Toby;
No rapture can equal the Tobyman's joys,
    To blue devil's blue plums (*j*) give the go-bye;
And what if, at length, boys, he come to the Crap (*k*),
    Even rack punch has *some* bitter in it,
For the Mare with three legs (*l.*) boys, I care not a rap,
    'T will be over in less than a minute!

GRAND CHORUS.

Then hip, hurrah!
Fling care away!
Hurrah for the game of High Toby!

Bess was the sole occupant of the apartment, and was applying herself to the task of learning a new ballad which had just emanated from the brain of some favorite poet in the purlieus of St Giles, and after a little study had committed it to memory so far, that by an occasional peep at the paper, she was enabled to warble forth the following song:—

THE SCAMPSMAN.

I.

THERE is not a king, should you search the world round,
So blithe as the king of the Road to be found;
His pistol's his sceptre, his saddle's his throne,
Whence he levies supplies, or enforces a loan.
                Derry Down.

II.

To this monarch the highway presents a wide field
Where each passing subject a tribute must yield;
His palace (the tavern) receives him at night,
Where sweet lips and sound liquor *crown* all with delight.
                Derry Down.

(*h*) Pocket book.   (*i*) Money.   (*j*) Bullets.   (*k*) The Gallows.   (*l*) Ditto.

III.

The soldier and sailor, both robbers by trade,
Full soon on the shelf, if disabled, are laid ;
The one gets a patch, and the other a peg,
But, while luck lasts, the highwayman shakes a loose leg !
Derry Down.

IV.

Most fowls rise at dawn, but the owl wakes at e'en,
And a jollier bird can there nowhere be seen ;
Like the owl, our snug Scampsman his snooze takes by day,
And when night draws her curtain scuds after his prey !
Derry Down.

V.

As the highwayman's life is the fullest of zest,
So the highwayman's death is the briefest and best ;
He dies not, as other men die, by *degrees*,—
But AT ONCE, without wincing, and quite at hs ease !
Derry Down

We have said that Bess was sitting alone ;—at the conclusion of her ditty she was disturbed by the sound of a footfall on the stairs, succeeded by a tap at the door of her room. She arose, but not without trepidation : her fears that a search would be made for her paramour, giving rise to constant anxiety. On admitting her visitor, she was agreeably disappointed in recognising the well known face of Jonathan Wild.

Jonathan's personal appearance was much improved ; as if the occasion of his visit to Edgeworth Bess had caused him to pay more attention to his toilet than was customary. Such indeed was the fact.

Jonathan had, it would seem, for some time past been smitten with the charms of Edgeworth Bess ; and although deeming it politic to resign her to Jack Sheppard, the more securely to bind him to his uses, he now was anxious to take the girl to himself, and with that view had visited her on the present occasion. Ceremony was dispensed with on his part, and he boldly told her his object ; urging on her attention the difference in the position she held as Sheppard's mistress, to that which she might command by placing herself under his protection.

Bess, with a constancy that under other circumstances would have been praiseworthy, repulsed the advances of Wild, and declared, that in life or death, her fate was firmly linked to that of the man she loved.

Jonathan Wild was unprepared for this humiliating refusal of what appeared in his eye a lowering of his own dignity ; and a feeling akin to hatred immediately took possession of his breast ;—for a few moments he remained silent.

"How's this?" at length exclaimed Jonathan ; "do you recollect that Jack's life is in my power—that at my will, his carcase would dangle from the triple tree ; do you recollect my power, and yet refuse my offer?"

"Question me not, but leave me," replied Bess. "You had better."

"Leave you!" echoed Wild, with a contemptuous laugh. "Not just yet."

"I am not unprotected," rejoined the girl. "There are people in the house," and she made towards the door, crying "help, help!"

"It won't do, Bess," said Wild, intercepting her progress. "So spare your breath ; come, come, be reasonable, and listen to me. Here, do you see this purse and ring? both shall be yours if you are only civil ; but resistance will avail you nothing here."

Jonathan secured the door, and throwing his purse upon the table, he approached Bess.

"Keep off, man!" exclaimed the girl, snatching up a knife. "Keep off, and tempt me not to ——."

"Tempt you —— to what?" exclaimed Wild, retreating a step.

"To protect myself from your violence, at every hazard," rejoined Bess, with the loook of an amazon.

Jonathan watched an opportunity, and darting at the girl, seized her arm, and forced the knife from her grasp ; a struggle ensued, in which Bess soon became exhausted, and being forced on her knee, exclaimed "Mercy ! have mercy on a defenceless woman !"

"Well," replied Wild, slightly relaxing his grasp, "let it pass ; the money, and the ring are yours, and you are mine ; here, put it on your finger."

"Never !" screamed Bess. Uttering a terrible imprecation, Wild endeavored to seize the poor girl by the throat. In the struggle her cap fell off. The ruffian caught hold of her hair, and held her fast. The chamber rang with her shrieks. But her cries, instead of moving her assailant's compassion, only added to his fury. Planting his knee against her side, he pulled her towards him ; in another moment, he would have executed his purpose, if an arm from behind had not felled him to the ground.

When Bess looked up, her eye met that of Jack Sheppard, whose opportune arrival, had saved her from the brutal violence of Jonathan. A single glance, sufficed to acquaint him with the position of affairs ; and his first impulse, was to sacrifice Wild to his vengeance.

Jonathan quickly recovered his feet ; and deadly were the glances exchanged by the two men.

Published by J. Clarke, Waterloo Place, M.

Printed by W. Clark, Knights bum.

"Hark ye," at length said Jonathan, somewhat calmly; "you have thwarted me, but my revenge is certain: I swear to hang you, and I'll keep my word."

"Monster!" exclaimed Jack, clutching the knife: but Bess clung round his neck, and prevented any further violence.

"The murder of the merchant shall be disclosed," continued Wild; "I'll give you up; and on the gallows shall you confess the power and vengeance of Jonathan Wild!"

Jack endeavored to disengage himself from Bess, and get at Jonathan; but in an instant the thief-taker darted out of the room.

CHAPTER XII.

JACK'S ARREST.

EDGEWORTH BESS in vain urged Sheppard to fly to some place of safety, where he might be out of the reach of Wild's revenge; but Jack knew as little of fear as of honesty, and boldly declared his determination to await any proceedings Jonathan might adopt.

He was not long kept in suspense; for, towards the evening, Jonathan Wild, accompanied by three constables, entered the room armed, with a warrant for his arrest on the charge of murder, and implicating Bess as an accessary.

"You see, I am as good as my word," said Wild: "you will be a cleverer fellow than I take you for, if you slip through my fingers. You have been useful to me," said he, in an under tone; "but you have thwarted—have defied me, and I swear to hang you like a dog!"

"Villain!" involuntarily muttered Bess, as she tightly grasped Jack Sheppard's arm.

"Silence, my girl," said Jack, kindly; "fear nothing; Jack Sheppard is a match for Jonathan Wild any day."

They were hurried before a magistrate, and charged by Wild with the robbery and murder; but as Jack Sheppard stated that he had most important disclosures to make, as well as charges to bring forward against his accuser, he was committed with his female companion to the New Prison in Clerkenwell for further examination.

PUBLISHER'S NOTE

pp.34-35 are missing.

Once over the iron spikes, Bess exhibited no reluctance to be let down on the other side of the wall. Having seen his mistress safe down, Jack instantly descended.

And thus he effected his escape from the New Prison.

CHAPTER XIV.

JACK VISITS HIS MOTHER.

HAVING effected this daring exploit, our hero deemed it unsafe to be seen in London: and having instructed Edgeworth Bess to make her way to the Mint, and hide until he came to her, Jack determined on visiting his mother, and accordingly directed his steps towards Willesden.

As Jack opened the gate, and crossed the little garden, which exhibited in every part the neatness and attention of its owner, he almost trembled at the idea of further disturbing her peace of mind. Pausing with the intention of turning back, he glanced in the direction of the village church, the tower of which could just be seen through the trees. The rooks were cawing amid the boughs, and all nature appeared awaking to happiness.

After knocking for some time at the door without effect, he tried the latch, and to his surprise found it open. He stepped in with a heavy foreboding of calamity. A cat came and rubbed herself against him as he entered the house, and seemed by her mewing to ask him for food. That was the only sound he heard.

Jack was almost afraid of speaking; but at length he summoned courage to call out " Mother !"

" Who 's there ? " asked a faint voice from the bed.

" Your son," answered the boy.

" Jack ! " exclaimed the widow, starting up and drawing back the curtain. Is it indeed you, or am I dreaming ?"

" You 're not dreaming, mother," he answered. " I 'm come to say good bye to you, and to assure you of my safety before I leave this place."

Published by T. Kelly, 17 Paternoster Row Oct. 17.

Printed by W. Clerk 202 High Holborn.

K.

" Where are you going ? " asked his mother.

" I hardly know," returned Jack ; " but it 's not safe for me to remain much longer here."

" True," replied the widow, upon whom terrible recollections crowded, " I know it is n't. I won't keep you long. But tell me how have you escaped from the confinement in which you were placed—come and sit by me—here— upon the bed—give me your hand—and tell me all about it."

Her son complied, and sat down upon the patch-work coverlet beside her.

" Jack," said Mrs Sheppard, clasping him with a hand that burnt with fever, " I have been ill—dreadfully ill—I believe delirious—I thought I should have died last night—I won't tell you what agony you have caused me—I won't reproach you. Only promise me to amend—to quit your vile companions— and I will forgive you—will bless you. Oh ! my dear, dear son, be warned in time. You are in the hands of a wicked, a terrible man, who will not stop till he has completed your destruction. Listen to your mother's prayers, and do not let her die broken-hearted."

" It is too late," returned Jack, sullenly ; " I can't be honest, if I would," and he started on his feet and grasped his hat.

" Oh ! do not say so," replied his wretched parent. " It is never too late. I hear you are in Jonathan Wild's power. Beware of him, my son ! Beware of him ! You know not what villany he is capable of. Be honest, and you will be happy. Though you have strayed from the right path, a stronger hand than your own has led you thence. Return, I implore of you—acknowledge your faults. God is all kindness, and will overlook them for your poor mother's sake. Return to him, I say—"

" I can't," replied Jack, doggedly.

" Can't ! " repeated his mother. " Why not ?"

" I am a robber, a murderer ! " replied Jack, heedless of the effect this dis- closure from his own lips might have upon his parent. " The blood hounds of the law are on my track ; nothing but death awaits me, if I am taken. But I have done them yet—I have escaped ! ha, ha !

Mrs. Sheppard had not heard the conclusion of her son's wild raving ; but at the mention of the murder, she uttered a shriek, and fell back upon the bed senseless.

Jack was at a loss how to act ; he almost feared to stop in the cottage, and yet could not tear himself from his mother's inanimate body. In vain he tried the various means his fancy prompted, to restore her, all were vain. A death-like coldness pervaded his frame—and in a frenzy, Jack loudly accused himself of being his mother's murderer.

His frantic exclamations, attracted the attention of an old woman, who was passing near the cottage ; and approaching the door, she met Jack, who was rushing forth to seek assistance. Accompanied by the woman, Jack re-entered the cottage, and directing that every care should be taken to restore his parent, he hastened from the place, absorbed in grief.

CHAPTER XV.

JACK SHEPPARD IN HIS GLORY.

It will readily be conceived, that a youth of the disposition we have recorded, as belonging to Jack Sheppard, was utterly incapable of receiving any lasting impression, from the scene described in the previous chapter.

Jack bent his steps towards the Mint, but took a circuitous route, the better to elude the vigilance of the authorities ; who, he knew would discover his flight at an early hour in the morning, and cause an immediate search for him. He reached the Mint in safety, and was joyously welcomed by Edgeworth Bess, and its inhabitants.

All feelings of remorse vanished, when Jack found himself in the arms of Bess, and the *hero* of the circle that surrounded him. He forgot, altogether, the anguish of his mother, and his own peril, and at once resigned himself to revelry and mirth.

The daring exploit of escaping with his mistress, from the New Prison of Clerkenwell, caused Jack's name to be applauded to the utmost, and no honor that the 'Minters' could devise, was neglected to be offered to them. The men vied with each other in enthusiastic praise ; and the women envied Edgeworth Bess her good fortune, in being the 'loved one' of such a daring fellow.

Much liquor was drank, in toasting the happy pair ; and during the evening, Jack favored the company with the following flash song :—

NIX MY DOLL, PALS, FAKE AWAY.

I.

In a box (*a*) of the Stone Jug (*b*) I was born,
Of a hempen widow (*c*) the kid forlorn.

Fake away.

And my father, as I've heard say,

Fake away.

Was a merchant of capers (*d*) gay,
Who cut his last fling with great applause,

(*e*) *Nix my doll, pals, fake away.*

II.

Who cut his last fling with great applause
To the tune of a " hearty choke with caper sauce."

Fake away.

The knucks in quod (*f*) did my schoolmen play,

Fake away.

And put me up to the time of day ;
Until at last there was none so knowing,

Nix my doll, pals, fake away.

III.

Until at last there was none so knowing,
No such sneaksman (*g*) or buzgloak (*h*) going,

Fake away.

Fogles (*i*) and fawnies (*j*) soon went their way,

Fake away.

To the spout (*k*) with the sneezers (*l*) in grand array,
No dummy hunter (*m*) had forks (*n*) so fly ;

Nix my doll, pals, fake away.

IV.

No dummy hunter had forks so fly,
No knuckler (*o*) so deftly could fake a cly (*p*),

Fake away.

No slour'd hoxter (*q*) my snipes (*r*) could stay,

Fake away.

(*a*) Cell. (*b*) Newgate. (*c*) A woman whose husband has been hanged. (*d*) A dancing master. (*e*) " Nothing comrades on on, supposed to be addressed by a thief to his confederates. (*f*) Thieves in prison. (*g*) Shoplifter. (*h*) Pickpocket. (*i*) Handkerchiefs. (*j*) Rings. (*k*) To the Pawnbroker. (*l*) Snuff boxes. (*m*) Pickpocket. (*n*) The two forefingers used in picking a pocket. (*o*) Pickpocket. (*p*) Pick a pocket. (*q*) No inside coat pocket, buttoned up. (*r*) Scissars.

None knap a reader (*s*) like me in the Lay.
Soon then I mounted in Swell-Street high.

>   *Nix my doll, pals, fake away*

V.

Soon then I mounted in Swell-Street high
And sported my flashiest toggery, (*t*)

>   *Fake away.*

Firmly resolved I would make my hay,

>   *Fake away.*

While mercury's star shed a single ray,
And ne'er was there seen such a dashing prig (*u*),

>   *Nix my doll, pals, fake away.*

VI.

And ne'er was there seen such a dashing prig,
With my strummel faked in the newest twig (*v*)

>   *Fake away.*

With my fawnied famms (*w*) and my onions gay (*x*)

>   *Fake away.*

My thimble of ridge (*y*), and my driz kemesa (*z*)
All my togs were so niblike (*aa*) and splash,

>   *Nix my doll, pals, fake away.*

VII.

All my togs were so niblike and splash,
Readily the queer screens I then could smash (*bb*) :

>   *Fake away.*

But my nuttiest blowen (*cc*), one fine day,

>   *Fake away.*

To the beaks (*dd*) did her fancy man betray,
And thus I was bowled out at last (*ee*).

>   *Nix my doll, pals, fake away-*

VIII.

And thus I was bowled out at last,
And into the Jug for a lag was cast (*ff*);

>   *Fake away.*

But I slipped my darbies (*gg*) one morn in May,

>   *Fake away.*

And gave to the dubsman (*hh*) a holiday,

And here I am pals, merry and free,

A regular rollocking Romany (*ii*).

>   *Nix my doll, pals, fake away.*

(*s*) Steal a pocket book.   (*t*) Best made clothes.   (*u*) **Thief.**   (*v*) With my hair dressed in the first fashion.
(*w*) With several rings on my hands.   (*x*) Seals.   (*y*) Gold **watch.**   (*z*) Laced shirt.   (*aa*) Gentlemanlike.   (*bb*
Easily then forged notes could I pass.   (*cc*) Favorite mistress.   (*dd*) Police.   (*ee*) Taken at length.   (*ff*) Cas
for transportation.   (*gg*) Fetters.   (*hh*) Turnkey.   (*ii*) Gipsy.

JACK ESCAPING FROM THE CONDEMNED HOLD IN NEWGATE

1.

Uproarious applause followed Jack's performance, and noisy revelry maintained the ascendant until day-break.

Jack and Bess at length retired: and after sleeping off the effects of the night's debauch, they began to consider the best means of evading the search, which had already commenced for them.

After many suggestions on either side, Jack Sheppard determined on testing the generosity of the 'Minters,' to procure a supply of cash and new clothes for himself and Bess; and by shifting their lodging continually, he deemed it probable they might successfully preserve an *incognito*, until their prospects brightened. The 'Minters' did not fall short of Jack's anticipations; and in the evening, he was master of a good sum of money and a suit of clothes, that had once belonged to an 'exquisite of the first water.'

In justice to our hero, we must record that he well became his smart apparel, and presented an appearance, when thus dressed, that would have passed muster in any society. The reader will therefore readily fancy, that in the eyes of Edgeworth Bess, he appeared little less than a paragon.

It was decided by the more cautious of Jack's friends, that he should leave the 'Mint' that night, and take up his lodging in one of the night cellars, which abounded in London, at the period of this history.

Accordingly in the dusk of evening, Jack left the 'Mint,' and bent his steps towards Thames Street; the main streets of the metropolis were then but imperfectly lighted, while the less-frequented avenues were left in total obscurity; but, even at the present time, the maze of courts and alleys into which Jack plunged, would have perplexed any one, not familiar with their intricacies, to thread them on a dark night. Sheppard, however, was well acquainted with the road. Indeed, it was his boast that he could find his way through any part of London blindfolded; and by this time, it would seem, he had nearly arrived at his destination; for, grasping his companion's arm, he led her along a narrow entry which did not appear to have an outlet, and came to a halt. Cautioning Bess, if she valued her neck, to tread carefully, Jack then descended a steep flight of steps; and, having reached the bottom in safety, he pushed open a door, that swung back on its hinges as soon as it had admitted him; and, followed by the girl, entered the night-cellar.

The vault, in which our hero found himself, resembled in some measure the cabin of a ship. It was long and narrow, with a ceiling supported by huge uncovered rafters, and so low as scarcely to allow him to stand erect beneath it. Notwithstanding the heat of the season,—which was not, however, found particularly inconvenient in this subterranean region,—a large heaped-up fire blaze ruddily in one corner, and lighted up a circle of as villanous countenances as ever flame shone upon.

The guests congregated within the night-cellar were, in fact, little better than thieves ; but thieves who confined their depredations almost exclusively to the vessels lying in the pool and docks of the river. They had as many designations as grades. There were game watermen and game lightermen, heavy horsemen and light horsemen, scuffle-hunters, and long-apron men, lumpers, journeymen coopers, mud-larks, badgers, and rat-catchers—a race of dangerous vermin, at this period flourishing in vast numbers. Besides these plunderers, there were others with whom the disposal of their pillage necessarily brought them into contact, and who seldom failed to attend them during their hours of relaxation and festivity ;—to wit, dealers in junk, old rags, and marine stores, purchasers of prize-money, crimps, and Jew receivers. The latter formed by far the most knavish-looking and unprepossessing portion of the assemblage. One or two of the tables were occupied by groups of fat frowzy women in flat caps, with rings on their thumbs, and baskets by their sides ; and no one who had listened for a single moment to their coarse language and violent abuse of each other, would require to be told they were fish-wives from Billingsgate.

The mistress of this cellar was a comely middle-aged dame, almost as stout, and quite as shrill-voiced, as the Billingsgate fish-wives above-mentioned. She had a warm nut-brown complexion, almost as dark as a Creole ; and a moustache on her upper lip, that would have done no discredit to the oldest dragoon in the King's service. This lady was singularly lucky in her matrimonial connexions. She had been married four times : three of her husbands having died of hempen fevers.

On the appearance of the fugitives, she was standing near the fire superintending some culinary preparation ; but she no sooner perceived them, than hastily quitting her occupation, she elbowed a way through the crowd, and ushered them, with much ceremony, into an inner room. Jack briefly stated to the hostess that circumstances compelled him to avail himself of the sanctuary her cellar afforded, and assuring her that he intended faring well and was prepared to pay liberally, at once won her to his services. In this night-cellar did Jack Sheppard and Edgworth Bess pass several happy days.

CHAPTER XVI.

JACK VISITS HIS MOTHER IN BEDLAM.

AFTER a lapse of some weeks, Jack Sheppard felt an overpowering wish to learn the fate of his mother: who, it will be remembered, he left in a state of insensibility at her cottage at Willesden.

After many enquiries, he at length heard that so violent had been the shock her feelings had sustained at their last interview, that reason had vacated her seat, and the wretched woman had been removed by some charitable individuals to Old Bedlam.

Jack immediately came to the determination of seeing his parent once more; and, despite the opposition of Edgeworth Bess, whose love for him conjured up various pictures of his capture by the officers, prepared to start at once.

"Risk, or no risk," said Jack, "I am resolved to see her without delay."

"It's a hopeless job," grumbled Bess, "and harm will come of it. What are you to do with a mad mother at a time when you need all your wits to take care of yourself?"

"Don't concern yourself further about it." returned Jack. "Once for all, I shall go."

"Won't you take me?" enquired Bess.

"No; you must await my return here."

"Then I must wait a long time," grumbled she. "You'll never return."

"We shall see," replied Jack. And having partaken of a hasty meal, he set out.

Old Bethlehem, or Bedlam,—every trace of which has been swept away, and the hospital for lunatics removed to Saint George's Field,—was a vast and magnificent structure. Erected in Moorfields in 1675, upon the model of the Tuileries, it is said that Louis the Fourteenth was so incensed at the insult offered to his palace, that he had a counterpart of St James's built for offices of the meanest description. The size and grandeur of the edifice, indeed drew down the ridicule of several of the wits of the age: by one of whom— the facetious Tom Brown—it was said, "Bedlam is a pleasant place, and abounds with amusements ;—the first of which is the building, so stately a fabric for persons wholly insensible of the beauty and use of it : the outside being a perfect mockery of the inside, and admitting two amusing queries,—Whether the persons that ordered the building of it, or those that inhabit it, were the maddest? and, whether the name and thing be not as disagreeable as harp and harrow." By another—the no less facetious Ned Ward—it was termed, " a costly college for a crack-brained society, raised in a mad age, when the chief of the city were in a great danger of losing their senses, and so contrived it the more noble for their own reception ; or they would never have flung away so much money to so foolish a purpose." The cost of the building exceeded seventeen thousand pounds. However the taste of the architecture may be questioned, which was the formal French style of the period, the general effect was imposing. Including the wings, it presented a frontage of five hundred and forty feet. Each wing had a small cupola ; and, in the centre of the pile rose a larger dome, surmounted by a gilded ball and vane. The asylum was approached by a broad gravel walk, leading through a garden edged on either side by a stone balustrade, and shaded by tufted trees. A wide terrace then led to large iron gates, over which were placed the two celebrated figures of Raving and Melancholy Madness, executed by the elder Cibber, and commemorated by Pope in the Dunciad, in the well-known lines :—

> " Close to those walls where folly holds her throne,
> And laughs to think Monroe would take her down,
> Where, o'er the gates, by his famed father's hand,
> *Great Cibber's brazen, brainless brothers stand.*"

Internally, it was divided by two long galleries, one over the other. These galleries were separated in the middle by iron grates. The wards on the right were occupied by male patients, on the left by the females. In the centre of the upper gallery was a spacious saloon, appropriated to the governors of the asylum. But, the besetting evil of the place, and that which drew down the severest censures of the writers above-mentioned, was that this spot,—which of all others should have been most free from such intrusion—was made a public exhibition. There all the loose characters thronged, assignations were openly made, and the spectators diverted themselves with the vagaries of its miserable inhabitants.

Entering the outer gate, and traversing the broad gravel walk before mentioned, Jack ascended the steps, and was admitted, on feeing the porter, by another iron gate, into the hospital. Here he was almost stunned by the

Published by E. Grier Water Iroine Fleet St.

W. Clerk tab: 70 % High Holborn

M.

JACK AT HIS MOTHERS GRAVE.

deafening clamour resounding on all sides. Some of the lunatics were rattling their chains; some shrieking; some singing; some beating with frantic violence against the doors. Altogether, it was the most dreadful noise he had ever heard. Amidst it all, however, there were several light-hearted and laughing groups walking from cell to cell, to whom all this misery appeared matter of amusement. The doors of several of the wards were thrown open for these parties, and as Jack passed, he could not help glancing at the wretched inmates. Here was a poor half-naked creature, with a straw crown on his head, and a wooden sceptre in his hand, seated on the ground with all the dignity of a monarch on his throne. There was a mad musician, seemingly rapt in admiration of the notes he was extracting from a child's violin. Here was a terrific figure gnashing his teeth, and howling like a wild beast;—there a lover, with hands clasped together, and eyes turned passionately upward. In this cell was a huntsman, who had fractured his skull while hunting, and was perpetually hallowing after the hounds;—in that, the most melancholy of all, the grinning gibbering lunatic, the realization of " moody madness, laughing wild."

Hastening from this heart-rending spectacle, Jack soon reached the grating that divided the men's compartment from that appropriated to the women. Inquiring for Mrs Sheppard, a matron offered to conduct him to her cell.

" You'll find her quiet enough to-day, sir," observed the woman, as they walked along; " but she has been very outrageous latterly. Her nurse says she may live some time; but she seems to me to be sinking fast."

" Heaven help her!" sighed Jack. " I hope not."

" Her release would be a mercy," pursued the matron. " Oh! sir, if you'd seen her as I've seen her, you'd not wish for a continuance of misery."

As Jack made no reply, the woman proceeded.

" They say her son is to be hanged. I'm glad of it, I'm sure; for it is all owing to him his poor mother's here. See what crime does, sir. Those who act wickedly bring misery on all connected with them. And so gentle as the poor creature is, when she's not in her wild fits—it would melt a heart of stone to see her. She will cry days and nights together. If Jack Sheppard could behold his mother in this state, he'd have a lesson he'd never forget— ay, and a severer one than even the hangman could read him. Hardened as he may be, that would touch him. But he has never been near her— never."

Rambling in this way, the matron at length came to a halt, and taking out a key, pointed to a door and said, " This is Mrs Sheppard's ward, sir."

"Leave us together, my good woman," said Jack, putting a guinea into her hand.

"As long as you please, sir," answered the matron, dropping a curtsey. "There, sir," she added, unlocking the door, "you can go in. Do n't be frightened of her. She 's not mischievous—and besides she 's chained, and can't reach you."

So saying, she retired, and Jack entered into the cell.

Prepared as he was for a dreadful shock, and with his nerves strung to endure it, Jack absolutely recoiled before the appalling object that met his gaze. Cowering in a corner upon a heap of straw sat his unfortunate mother, the complete wreck of what she had been. Her eyes glistened in the darkness— for light was only admitted through a small grated window—like flames, and, as she fixed them on him, their glances seemed to penetrate his very soul. A piece of old blanket was fastened across her shoulders, and she had no other clothing except a petticoat. Her arms and feet were uncovered, and of almost skeleton thinness. Her features were meagre, and ghastly white, and had the fixed and horrible stamp of insanity. Her head had been shaved, and around it was swathed a piece of rag, in which a few straws were stuck. Her thin fingers were armed with nails as long as the talons of a bird. A chain, riveted to an iron belt encircling her waist, bound her to the wall. The cell in which she was confined was about six feet long and four wide.

When Jack entered the cell, she was talking to herself in the muttering unconnected way peculiar to her distracted condition ; but, after her eye had rested on him some time, the fixed expression of her features relaxed, and a smile crossed them. This smile was more harrowing even than her former rigid look.

"You are an angel," she cried, with a look beaming with delight.

"Rather a devil," groaned her son, " to have done this."

"You are an angel, I said," continued the poor maniac; "and my Jack would have been like you, if he had lived. But he died when he was a child— long ago—long ago—long ago."

"Would he had done so!" cried Jack.

"A Gipsy told me if he grew up he would be hanged. She showed me a black mark under his ear, where the noose would be tied. And so I 'll tell you what I did—"

And she burst into a laugh that froze Jack's blood in his veins.

"What did you do?" he asked, in a broken voice.

"I strangled him—ha! ha! ha!—strangled him while he was at my breast —ha! ha!"—And then with a sudden and fearful change of look, she added,

"That's what has driven me mad. I killed my child to save him from the gallows—oh! oh! One man hanged in a family is enough. If I'd not gone mad, they would have hanged me."

"Poor soul!" ejaculated her son.

"I'll tell you a dream I had last night," continued the unfortunate being. "I was at Tyburn. There was a gallows erected, and a great mob round it—thousands of people, and all with white faces like corpses. In the midst of them there was a cart with a boy in it—and that boy was Jack—my son Jack—they were going to hang him. How the mob shouted and huzzaed—and I shouted too—ha! ha! ha!"

"Mother!" cried Jack, unable to endure this agonizing scene longer. "Don't you know me, mother?"

"Ah!" shrieked Mrs. Sheppard. "What's that?—Jack's voice!"

"It is," replied her son.

"The ceiling is breaking! the floor is opening! he is coming to me!" cried the unhappy woman.

"He stands before you," rejoined her son.

"Where?" she cried. "I can't see him, where is he?"

"Here," answered Jack.

"Are you his ghost, then?"

"No—no," answered Jack. "I am your most unhappy son."

"Let me touch you, then; let me feel if you are really flesh and blood," cried the poor maniac, creeping towards him on all fours.

Jack did not advance to meet her. He could not move; but stood like one stupified, with his face buried in his hands.

"Come to me!" cried the poor maniac, who had crawled as far as the chain would permit her,—"come to me!" she cried, extending her thin arm towards him.

Jack fell on his knees beside her.

"Who are you," inquired Mrs Sheppard, passing her hands over his face and gazing at him with a look that made him shudder.

"Your son," replied Jack,—"your miserable son."

"It is false," cried Mrs Sheppard. "You are not. Jack was not half your age when he died."

"Oh, God!" cried Jack, "she does not know me. Mother—dear mother!" he added clasping her in his arms. "Look at me again."

"Off!" she exclaimed, breaking from his embrace with a scream. "Don't touch me. I'll be quiet. I'll not speak of Jack. I won't dig his grave with my nails. Don't strip me quite. Leave me my blanket! I'm very cold at night.   Or, if you must take off my clothes, do n't dash cold water on my head.   It throbs cruelly."

" Horror !" cried Jack.

" Do n't scourge me," she cried, trying to hide herself in the farthest corner of the cell.   " The lash cuts to the bone.   I ca n't bear it.   Spare me, and I 'll be quiet—quiet—quiet!

" Mother !" said Jack, advancing towards her.

" Off !" she cried with a prolonged and piercing shriek.   And she buried herself beneath the straw, which she tossed above her head with the wildest gestures.

" I shall kill her if I stay longer," muttered her son, completely terrified.

While he was considering what would be best to do, the poor maniac, over whose bewildered brain another change had come, raised her head from under the straw, and, peeping round the room, asked in a low voice, " If they were gone ?"

" Who ?" replied Jack.

" The nurses," she answered.

" Do they treat you ill ?" asked her son.

" Hush !" she said, putting her lean fingers to her lips   Hush !—come hither, and I 'll tell you."

Jack approached her.

" Sit beside me," continued Mrs. Sheppard.   " And, now I 'll tell you what they do.   Stop ! we must shut the door, or they 'll catch us.   See !" she added, tearing the rag from her head,—" I had beautiful black hair once.   But they cut it all off."

" I shall go mad myself if I listen to her longer," said Jack, attempting to rise.   " I must go."

" Do n't stir, or they 'll chain you to the wall," said his mother, detaining him.   " Now, tell me why they brought you here ?"

" I came to see you, dear mother !" answered Jack.

" Mother !" she echoed,—" mother ! why do you call me by that name ?"

" Because you are my mother."

" What !" she exclaimed, staring eagerly in his face.   " Are you my son ? Are you Jack ?"

" I am," replied Jack.   " Heaven be praised she knows me at last."

" Oh, Jack !" cried his mother, falling upon his neck, and covering him with kisses.

" Mother, dear mother !" said Jack, bursting into tears.

JACK SHEPPARD IN THE CASTLE IN NEWGATE.

" You will never leave me," sobbed the poor woman, straining him to her breast.

" Never—never ! "

The words were scarcely pronounced, when the door was violently thrown open, and two men appeared at it.

" Ah ! " exclaimed Jack, starting to his feet.

" Just in time," said the first. " You are my prisoner, Jack Sheppard."

" You shall take my life first," rejoined Jack.

And, as he was about to put himself into a posture of defence, his mother clasped him in her arms.

The movement was fatal to her son. Taking advantage of his embarrassed position, the officers rushed upon him, and disarmed him.

Jack was immediately handcuffed ; and, amidst the most piercing shrieks of the maddened widow, was dragged away to Newgate.

CHAPTER XVII.

OLD NEWGATE.

THOUGH by no means so extensive or commodious as the modern prison, Old Newgate was a large and strongly-built pile. The body of the edifice stood on the south side of Newgate Street, and projected at the western extremity far into the area opposite Saint Sepulchre's Church. One small wing lay at the north of the gate, where Giltspur Street Compter now stands ; and the Press Yard, which was detached from the main building, was situated at the back of Phœnix Court. The south or principal front, looking *down* the Old Bailey, and not *upon it,* as is the case of the present structure, with its massive walls of roughened free stone,—in some places darkened by the smoke, in others blanched, by exposure to the weather,—its heavy projecting cornice, its unglazed doubly-grated windows, its gloomy porch decorated with fetters, and defended by an enormous iron door, had a stern and striking appearance. Over the Lodge, upon a dial was inscribed the appropriate motto, " *Venio*

No. 13.]   N

sicut fur." The Gate, which crossed Newgate Street, had a wide arch for carriages, and a postern, on the north side, for foot-passengers. Its architecture was richly ornamental, and resembled the style of a triumphal entrance to a capital, rather than a dungeon, having battlements and hexagonal towers, and being adorned on the western side with a triple range of pilasters of the Tuscan order, amid the intercolumniations of which were niches embellished with statues. The chief of these was a figure of Liberty, with a cat at her feet, in allusion to the supposed origin of its former founder, Sir Richard Wittington. On the right of the postern against the wall was affixed a small grating, sustaining the debtor's box. Some years after the date of this history, an immense ventilator was placed at the top of the Gate, with the view of purifying the prison, which, owing to its insufficient space, and constantly-crowded state, was never free from that dreadful and contagious disorder, now happily unknown, the gaol-fever. So frightful, indeed, were the ravages of this malady, to which debtors and felons were alike exposed, that its miserable victims were frequently carried out by cart-loads, and thrown into a pit in the burial-ground of Christ-church, without ceremony.

Old Newgate was divided into three separate prisons,—the Master's Side, the Common Side, and the Press Yard. The first of these, situated at the south of the building, with the exception of one ward over the gateway, was allotted to the better class of debtors, whose funds enabled them to defray their chamber-rent, fees, and garnish. The second, comprising the bulk of the gaol, and by many degrees worse in point of accommodation, having several dismal and noisome wards under ground, was common both to debtors and malefactors,—an association little favorable to the morals or comforts of the former, who, if they were brought there with any notions of honesty, seldom left with untainted principles. The last,—in all respects the best and airiest of the three, standing, as has been before observed, in Phœnix Court, at the rear of the main fabric,—was reserved for state-offenders.

The Cellar was a large low-roofed vault, about four feet below the level of the street, perfectly dark, unless when illumined by a roaring fire, and candles stuck in pyramidal lumps of clay, with a range of butts and barrels at one end, and benches and tables at the other, where the prisoners, debtors and male-factors, male and female, assembled as long as their money lasted, and consumed the time in drinking, smoking, and gaming with cards and dice. Above was a spacious hall, connected with it by a flight of stone steps, at the further end of which stood an immense grated door, called in the slang of the place "The Jigger," through the bars of which the felons in the upper wards were allowed to converse with their friends, or if they wishedto enter the room, or join the revellers below, they were at liberty to do so, on payment of a small fine.

Two large wards were situated in the Gate; one of which, the Stone Ward, appropriated to the master debtors, looked towards Holborn; the other called the Stone Hall, from a huge stone standing in the middle of it, upon which the irons of criminals under sentence of death were knocked off previously to their being taken to the place of execution, faced Newgate-street. Here the prisoners took exercise.

In an angle of the Stone Hall was the Iron Hold, a chamber containing a vast assortment of fetters and handcuffs of all weights and sizes. When any violent outrage was committed,—and such matters were of daily, sometimes hourly, occurrence,—a bell, the rope of which descended into the hall, brought the whole of the turnkeys to their assistance. A narrow passage at the north of the Stone Hall led to the Bluebeard's room of this enchanted castle, a place called Jack Ketch's Kitchen, it was a sort of cooking-room, with an immense fire-place flanked by a couple of cauldrons—because the quarters of persons executed for treason were there boiled by the hangman in oil, pitch, and tar, before they were affixed on the city gates, or on London Bridge. Above this revolting spot was the female debtor's ward; below it a gloomy cell, called Tangier; and, lower still, the Stone Hold, a most terrible and noisome dungeon, situated underground, and unvisited by a single ray of daylight. Built and paved with stone, without beds, or any other sort of protection from the cold, this dreadful hole, accounted the most dark and dismal in the prison, was made the receptacle of such miserable wretches as could not pay the customary fees. Adjoining it was the Lower Ward. It was only a shade better than the Stone Hold. Ascending the gate once more on the way back, we find over the Stone Hall another large room, called Debtors' Hall, facing Newgate-street, with " very good air and light." A little too much of the former, perhaps; as the windows being unglazed, the prisoners were subjected to severe annoyance from the weather and easterly winds.

Of the women felon's rooms nothing has yet been said. There were two. One called Waterman's Hall, a horrible place adjoining the postern under the gate, whence, through a small barred aperture, they solicited alms from the passengers: the other, a large chamber, denominated My Lady's Hold, was situated in the highest part of the gaol, at the northern extremity. Neither of these wards had beds, and the unforutnate inmates were obliged to take their rest on the oaken floor. The condition of the rooms was indescribably filthy and disgusting; nor were the habits of the occupants much more cleanly.

There were two Condemned Holds,—one for each sex. That for the men lay near the Lodge, with which it was connected by a dark passage. It was a large room, about twenty feet long and fifteen broad, and had an arched stone roof. In fact, it had been anciently the right hand postern under the gate leading towards the city. The floor was planked with oak, and covered with iron staples, hooks, and ring-bolts, with heavy chains attached to them. There was only one small grated window in this hold, which admitted but little light.

There were two places of punishment which merited some notice from their peculiarity. Into the first, denominated the Bilbowes,—a dismal place,— refractory prisoners were thrust, and placed in a kind of stocks, whence the name.

The second, the Press room, a dark close chamber, near Waterman's Hall, obtained its name from an immense wooden machine kept in it, with which such prisoners as refused to plead to their indictments were pressed to death— a species of inquisitorial torture not discontinued until so lately as the early part of the reign of George the Third, when it was abolished by an express statute.

The revolting torture effected in this room is worthy description. The sentence which doomed an unhappy wretch to suffer it ran as follows:—

" *Prisoner at the bar, you shall be taken to the prison from whence you came, and put into a mean room, stopped from the light; and shall there be laid on the bare ground, without any litter, straw, or other covering, and without any garment. You shall lie upon your back; your head shall be covered; and your feet bare. One of your arms shall be drawn to one side of the room, and the other arm to the other side; and your legs shall be served in the like manner. Then, there shall be laid upon your body as much iron, or stone as you can bear, and more. And the first day, you shall have three morsels of barley bread, without any drink; and the second day, you shall be allowed to drink as much as you can, at three times, of the water that is near to the prison-door, except running-water, without any bread. And this shall be your diet till you die."*

The Press Room was a small square chamber, walled and paved with stone. In each corner stood a stout square post reaching to the ceiling. To these a heavy wooden apparatus was attached, which could be raised or lowered at pleasure by pullies. In the floor were set four ring-bolts, about nine feet apart. The prisoner was thrown upon his back, and the executioner attached

Published by I. Glover, Water Lane, Fleet Street

Etch'd by W. Hugh Hobart

O.

JACK'S PROGRESS IN THE GREAT ESCAPE.

strong cords to his ankles and wrists, and fastened them tightly to the iron rings. This done, the pulley was unloosed, and the ponderous machine, which resembled a trough, slowly descended upon the prisoner's breast. The executioner then took two iron weights, each of a hundred pounds, and placed them in the press. If this seemed insufficient, another hundred weight was added. After this torture had been endured for an hour, a fourth weight was added. An appalling change was then perceptible. The veins in the prisoner's throat and forehead swelled and blackened; the eyes protruded from their sockets, and stared wildly; a thick damp gathered on his brow; blood gushed from his mouth, nostrils, and ears: but death frequently ensued before the contumacious culprit would utter a word,

We have been thus explicit in describing Old Newgate, because within its walls Jack Sheppard effected the most extraordinary acts of his life.

After being seized in Bedlam, Sheppard was immured in Newgate until he was tried on a charge of murder and robbery, found guilty, and sentenced to death.

Jack for a long time entertained hopes of a reprieve, but on the 31st of August, 1724, the dead warrant arrived, ordering him for execution along with several other malefactors on the following Friday.

Now that Jack Sheppard's fate seemed sealed, the curiosity of the sightseeing public to behold him was redoubled. The prison gates were besieged like a booth at a fair; and the Condemned Hold where he was confined, and to which visitors were admitted at the moderate charge of a *guinea a-head*, had quite the appearance of a show-room. So intense was the anxiety to see the notorious housebreaker, that a hundred guineas a-day was pocketed by the turnkeys.

In the preceding general survey of the prison, but little was said of the Lodge. It may be well, therefore, before proceeding farther, to describe it more minutely. It was approached from the street by a flight of broad stone steps, leading to a ponderous door, plated with iron, and secured on the inner side by huge bolts, and a lock, with wards of a prodigious size. A little within stood a second door, or rather wicket, lower than the first, but of equal strength, and surmounted by a row of sharp spikes. As no apprehension was entertained of an escape by this outlet,—nothing of the kind having been attempted by the boldest felon ever incarcerated in Newgate,—both doors were generally left open during the day-time. At six-o'clock, the wicket was shut; and at nine, the gaol was altogether locked up. Not far from the entrance, on the left, was a sort of screen, or partition-wall, reaching from the floor to the ceiling, formed of thick oaken planks riveted together by iron bolts, and studded with broad-headed nails. In this screen, which masked the entrance of a dark passage communicating with the Condemned Hold, about five feet from the ground, was a hatch, protected by long spikes set six inches apart : scarcely space enough for the passage of a hand being left between their points and the beam. Here, as has already been observed, condemned malefactors were allowed to hold converse with such of their guests as had not interest or money enough to procure admission to them in the hold. Beyond the hatch, an angle, formed by a projection in the wall of some three or four feet, served to hide a door conducting to the interior of the prison.

CHAPTER XVIII.

JACK'S ESCAPE FROM THE CONDEMNED HOLD.

On the arrival of the *dead warrant*, it would be presumed Jack Sheppard would have been awakened to the awfulness of the situation he filled ; but it was not so. Instead of being cast down, he appeared gayer than ever ; and when the head turnkey offered him ten guineas as a share of the receipts from his curious visitors, he gave it to the poor debtors and felons on the Common Side of the prison to drink his health.

Jack's most constant visitor was Edgeworth Bess, who had been examined on the charge of aiding him in his nefarious doings, and acquitted for want of conclusive evidence ; and with all the vigilence displayed by the keeper of the prison, she succeeded in supplying her lover with a watch spring file, with which he applied himself to one of the spikes of the hatch, and succeeded with much labor in getting it so far through, that his own strength was sufficient to snap it off. This final event was however deferred, until a favorable opportunity should present itself.

At length the day preceding that fixed for Jack's execution arrived, and in the evening he expressed a desire to be allowed the indulgence of a parting interview with Edgeworth Bess, after the usual time allowed by visitors.

The gaoler consented : but would only allow them to converse through the spikes, which secured the hatch; and seeing the intense grief with which Bess was afflicted, left her and a female companion, whom she had provided herself with, to take their last farewell of Jack uninterrupted.

This was more than Sheppard could have hoped for, in his most sanguine wishes to succeed in his escape.

" Now, dear Jack," exclaimed Bess. " Lose no time, fortune favors us — quick, quick! remove the bar." And she applied her strength to force the spike, while Jack pulled with all his might.

" Can't we break it off ? " earnestly enquired the woman, who accompanied Edgeworth Bess, and who was of a more masculine build.

" Let 's try again, at all events," replied Bess. And their united power was applied to the bar, while Jack seconded their efforts from within; after great exertions on both sides, the spike yielded to their combined strength, and snapped suddenly off.

" Holloa—what 's that ? " cried the gaoler, who was within hearing.

" Only my darbies," returned Jack, clinking his chains.

" Now, give me the woollen cloth to tie round my fetters," whispered Sheppard. " Quick."

" Here it is," replied Edgeworth Bess.

" Give me your hand, Poll, to help me through," cried Jack, as he accomplished the operation. " Keep a sharp look out, Bess."

" Stop ! " interposed Edgeworth Bess; " the man is coming this way. We 're lost."

" Help me through at all hazards, Poll," cried Jack, straining towards the opening.

" The danger 's past," whispered Bess. " He has gone again; we 're all safe."

" Do n't lose a moment then," cried Jack, forcing himself into the aperture, while the two women pulled him through it.

" There ! " cried Jack, as he reached the ground without noise ; " we 're safe so far."

" Come, my disconsolate darlings," cried the turnkey ; " it only wants five minutes to six. I expect the governor here presently. Cut it as short as you can."

" Only two minutes more, sir," intreated Edgeworth Bess, advancing towards him in such a manner as to screen Jack, who crept into the farthest part of the angle,—" only two minutes, and we 've done."

" Well, well, I 'm not within a minute," rejoined the turnkey.

" We shall never be able to get you out unseen, Jack," whispered Bess.
" You must make a bold push."

" Impossible," replied Sheppard, in the same tone.   " That would be certain
destruction.   I can't run in these heavy fetters.   No : I must face it out.
Tell your companion to slip out, and I 'll put on her cloak and hood."

Jack contrived to put on the hood and cloak, and being about the size of the
rightful owner, presented a very tolerable resemblance to her.   This done,
the woman, who watched her opportunity, slipped out of the Lodge.

" Halloa !" exclaimed the turnkey, who had caught a glimpse of her departing figure, is one of you women gone ?"

" No—no," hastily interposed Edgeworth Bess ; we 're both here.   Don't
you see we 're putting on our cloaks ?"

At this moment, Saint Sepulchre's clock struck six.

" Close the wicket, vociferated the goaler," in an authentic tone.

" Good bye !" cried Jack, as if taking leave of his mistresses.

" Good bye," replied Bess.   " Good bye, Jack ! Keep up your spirits."

" Now for it !—life or death !" exclaimed Jack, assuming the gait of a female,
and stepping towards the door.

Just as Jack gained the entrance, he heard the man's footstep behind him,
and aware that the slightest indiscretion would betray him, he halted, uncer-
tain what to do.

" Stop a minute, my dear," cried the goaler.   " You forget that you promised me a kiss the last time you were here."

" Won't one from me do as well ? " interposed Edgeworth Bess, as she
planted herself between Jack and the turnkey.   It was a moment of breathless
interest to all engaged in the attempt.

" As you like," cried the man, endeavoring to pass his arm familiarly round
the girl's waist.

" Hands off ! " she exclaimed, or you 'll repent it."

" Why, what 'll you do ? " demanded the turnkey.

" Teach you to keep your distance !" retorted Bess, dealing him a buffet
that sent him reeling several yards backwards.

" Off with you !" roared the discomfited fellow, "and, don't come here
again."

Before however he had recovered himself, Jack and Bess had disappeared.

Thus did Jack effect his first escape from Old Newgate.

W.Clerk Lith 202 High Holborn.

Published by J. Clement Wine Office Court.

P.

JACK'S ESCAPE FROM THE LEADS OF NEWGATE.

CHAPTER XIX.

JACK SHEPPARD LOSES HIS MOTHER.

ON quitting Newgate, Jack hurried into a vehicle that was waiting close by, and at a rapid pace was driven towards Rotherhithe; and under the roof of one of his companions, who had been apprised of the attempt that was to be made by Edgeworth Bess to deliver him from his bondage, he was eased of his fetters.

As it would have been madness in Jack to remain long in one place, he closely disguised himself, and ventured to walk abroad; judging rightly, that extraordinary exertions would be made to re-capture him; and, that if again lodged in Newgate, all hopes of another escape would vanish before the strict guard that would be placed over him.

During his rambles, Jack sat himself down at the front of an ale house door in St Giles's; and having called for some refreshment, was about to raise the cup to his lips, when he was checked by overhearing the following conversation pass amongst the idlers who were lounging near him.

"Awful end Jack Sheppard's mother come to. Suicide in a mad house is dreadful work. It's well they let her have Christian burial. They say she killed herself when she heard that her son's dead-warrant had gone to Newgate. The Crowner's 'quest sat on her yesterday: and if she had n't been proved out of her mind, she would have been buried in the cross-roads."

Jack almost fell from his seat, so suddenly did the intelligence of his mother's dreadful death come upon him. He however recovered himself sufficiently to prevent his emotions being observed by those near him, but the cup was placed untasted on the table.

With much eagerness did Jack now try to catch every word that was uttered concerning his lost parent; and, amongst other things, gathered that the funeral was to take place on the following day at the parish Church of Willesden: such being the dying request of the unfortunate woman.

Having heard thus much, Sheppard hastened from the spot, and wandered about careless as to the direction he took.

Bitter were the pangs that rent the housebreaker's heart, as he reflected that he was the cause of his mother's death, if not actually her murderer. And he was nigh falling from excessive grief, when he found relief in a flood of tears.

Jack determined to be present at the ceremony on the morrow; and prepared himself to pay the only reverence to his dead mother now in his power, by appearing in a garb of mourning.

That night Jack walked to Paddington, and took up his quarters at a small tavern called the Wheatsheaf, near the green. On the next morning, he set out along the Harrow Road.

It was a clear, lovely morning. The air was sharp and bracing, and the leaves which had taken their autumnal tints were falling from the trees. The road which wound by Westbourne Green, gave him a full view of the hill of Hampstead, with its church, its crest of houses, and its villas peeping from out the trees.

Jack's heart was too full to allow him to derive any pleasure from this scene; so he strolled on without raising his eyes till he arrived at Kensal Green, and mounting the hill turned off into the fields on the right. Crossing them, he ascended an eminence, which, from its singular shape, seems to have been the site of a Roman encampment, and which commands a magnificent prospect.

Leaning upon a gate he looked down into the valley, and beheld the grey tower of Willesden Church, embosomed in its grove of trees, now clothed in all the glowing livery of autumn. There was the cottage his mother had inhabited for so many years,—in those fields she had rambled,—at that church she had prayed. And he had destroyed all this. But for him she might have been alive and happy. The recollection was too painful, and he burst into an agony of tears.

Hastening to the church, he entered it by the very door near which his *first theft* had been committed. Shrinking involuntarily back into the farthest corner of the seat, Jack buried his face in his hands, The service began. Jack, who had not been in a place of worship for many years, was powerfully affected.

Returning to the churchyard, he walked round it; and on the western side, near a small yew-tree, discovered a new made grave; 't was for his mother.

At this moment, the bell began to toll in a peculiar manner, announcing the approach of the corpse. The coffin was brought into the churchyard; and Jack, whose eyes were filled with tears, followed at a foot's space behind the melancholy procession; which consisted of only two mourners—two men who had known and respected the poor widow.

Jack had been touched in the morning, but he was now completely prostrated. In the midst of the holy place, which he had formerly profaned, lay the body of his unfortunate mother, and he could not help looking upon her untimely end as the retributive vengeance of Heaven for the crime he had committed. His grief was so audible, that it attracted the notice of some of the bystanders.

The funeral procession had now approached the grave, around which many who were deeply interested by the sad ceremonial had gathered. The clergyman proceeded with the service, while the coffin was deposited at the brink of the grave.

Just as the attendants were preparing to lower the corpse into the earth, Jack fell on his knees beside the coffin, uttering the wildest exclamations of grief, reproaching himself with the murder of his mother, and invoking the vengeance of heaven on his own head.

A murmur ran through the assemblage, by several of whom Jack was recognised. But such was the violence of his grief,—such the compunction he exhibited, that they looked on with an eye of compassion.

Jack's grief was permitted to flow uninterrupted; and at length the coffin was lowered into the earth, and the venerable clergyman retired.

Much anxiety was now evinced amongst the crowd as to the necessity of seizing the escaped convict; and a handbill, offering a reward of five hundred pounds to any one who would deliver him at Newgate, was produced, and served to stimulate the villagers in their determination to seize Sheppard.

Room was however made for the parish constable, who came bustling up with his heavy staff in his hand; and, approaching Jack who had remained transfixed by the side of the grave, exclaimed, " You are my prisoner!"

Jack started to his feet; but before he could defend himself, he was closed upon by the villagers, whose superior numbers rendered resistance powerless: and after being securely bound hand and foot, he was fastened into the bottom of a cart, and driven towards town with an escort of well armed countrymen.

CHAPTER XX.

JACK SHEPPARD AGAIN IN NEWGATE.

THE arrest of Jack Sheppard was rendered complete by his safe delivery at Newgate; and the governor, in order to prevent all possibility of his again escaping, had him conveyed to the apartment known as *The Castle*, and considered from its position to be the most secure of any in the prison.

Jonathan Wild exerted his influence to render the prisoner's sufferings as severe as possible; and at his suggestion Jack was subjected to a course of privation hitherto unknown even in Newgate.

As soon as it became known, through the medium of the public prints on the following day, that Jack Sheppard had been again captured, fresh curiosity was excited, and larger crowds than ever flocked to Newgate, in the hope of obtaining admission to his cell; but by the governor's express commands, no one was allowed to see him. He was removed from *The Castle*, stripped of his fine apparel, clothed in the most sordid rags, loaded with additional fetters, and thrust into the Stone Hold, already described as the most noisome cell in the whole prison. Here, without a glimpse of daylight; visited by no one; fed upon the worst diet, literally mouldy bread and ditch-water: surrounded by stone walls; with a flagged floor for his pillow, and without so much as a blanket to protect him from the death-like cold that pierced his frame,—Jack's stout heart was subdued, and he fell into the deepest dejection, ardently longing for the time when even a violent death should terminate his sufferings. But it was not so ordered.

A question arose whether the prisoner could be executed under the existing warrant,—some inclining to one opinion, some to another. The most eminent lawyers of the day, however, decided that it must be proved in a regular and judicial manner that Sheppard was the identical person who had been convicted and had escaped, before a fresh order could be made for his execution;

JACK'S CHAINS KNOCK'D OFF.

Published by I. Fairburn, Water Lane, Fleet St.

W Clark delt 209 Highholborn.

and that the matter must, therefore, stand over until the next sessions, to be held at the Old Bailey in October, when it could be brought before the court.

Sheppard meanwhile, who was not informed of the respite, languished in his horrible dungeon, and, at the expiration of three weeks, became so seriously indisposed, that it was feared he could not long survive. He refused his food, —and even when better provisions were offered him, rejected them. As his death was by no means desired by the mercenary turnkeys, they resolved to remove him to a more airy ward, and afford him such slight comforts as might tend to his restoration, or at least to keep him alive until the period of his execution. With this view, Jack was carried—for he was no longer able to move without assistance, back to *The Castle*. The walls were of immense thickness ; the small windows were *doublegrated* and unglazed. It was about twelve feet high, nine wide, and fourteen long ; and was approached by double doors each six inches thick. As Jack appeared to be sinking fast, his fetters were removed, his own clothes were restored to him, and he was allowed a mattress and a scanty supply of bedlinen. Under this treatment he speedily revived. And as soon as he became convalescent, he was again loaded with irons ; fastened by an enormous horse-padlock to a staple in the floor ; and only allowed to take repose in a chair. A single blanket constituted his whole covering at night. In spite of all this, he grew daily better and stronger, and his spirits revived. Still, no visitors were permitted to see him. In this way, more than a month passed over. October arrived ; and in another week the court would be sitting at the Old Bailey.

One afternoon at three o'clock, the turnkey brought up Jack's provisions, and, after carefully examining his fetters, and finding all secure, told him if he wanted anything further he must mention it, as he should not be able to return in the evening, his presence being required elsewhere. Jack replied in the negative, and it required all his mastery over himself to prevent the satisfaction which this announcement afforded him from being noticed by the gaoler, who after a scrutinizing glance around departed.

" Now," cried Jack, leaping up, " for an achievement, compared with which all I have yet done shall be as nothing ! "

CHAPTER XXI.

JACK'S GREAT ESCAPE!

JACK SHEPPARD's first object was to free himself from his handcuffs. This he accomplished by holding the chain that connected them firmly between his teeth, and squeezing his fingers as closely together as possible, succeeded in drawing his wrists through the manacles. He next twisted the heavy gyves round and round, and partly by main strength, partly by a dexterous and well-applied jerk, snapped asunder the central link by which they were attached to the padlock. Taking off his stockings, he then drew up the basils as far as he was able, and tied the fragments of the broken chain to his legs, to prevent them from clanking, and impeding his future exertions.

Jack discovered that his course up the chimney was obstructed by an iron bar. To remove this obstacle it was necessary to make an extensive breach in the wall. With the broken links of the chain, which served him in lieu of more efficient implements, he commenced operations just above the chimney-piece, and soon contrived to pick a hole in the plaster.

He found the wall, as he suspected, solidly constructed of brick and stone : and with the slight and inadequate tools which he possessed, it was a work of infinite labor and skill to get out a single brick. That done, however, he was well aware the rest would be comparaively easy.

Animated by this trifling success, he proceeded with fresh ardor, and the rapidity of his progress was proclaimed by the heap of bricks, stones, and mortar which before long covered the floor. At the expiration of an hour, by dint of unremitting exertion, he had made so large a breach in the chimney, that he could stand upright in it. He was now within a foot of the bar, and introducing himself into the hole, speedily worked his way to it.

Regardless of the risk he incurred from some heavy stone dropping on his head or feet, - regardless also of the noise made by the falling rubbish, and of the imminent danger which he consequently ran of being interrupted by some of the gaolers, should the sound reach their ears, he continued to pull down large masses of the wall, which he flung upon the floor of the cell.

Having worked thus for another quarter of an hour without being sensible of fatigue, though he was half stifled by the clouds of dust which his exertions raised, he had made a hole about three feet wide, and six high, and uncovered the iron bar. Grasping it firmly with both hands, he quickly wrenched it from the stones in which it was mortised, and leapt to the ground. On examination, it proved to be a flat bar of iron, nearly a yard in length, and more than an inch square.

While he was examining the bar, he fancied he heard the lock tried. A chill ran through his frame, and, grasping the heavy weapon with which chance had provided him, prepared to strike down the first person who should enter the cell. After listening attentively for a short time without drawing breath, he became convinced that his apprehensions were groundless, and, greatly relieved, sat down upon the chair to rest himself and prepared for further efforts.

Acquainted with every part of the gaol, Jack well knew that his only chance of effecting an escape must be by the roof. To reach it would be a most difficult undertaking. Still it was possible, and the difficulty was only a fresh incitement.

The mere enumeration of the obstacles that existed would have deterred any spirit less daring than Sheppard's from even hazarding the attempt. Independently of other risks, and of the chance of breaking his neck in the descent, he was aware that to reach the leads he should have to break open six of the strongest doors of the prison. Armed, however, with the implement he had so fortunately obtained, he did not despair of success.

Burning to be avenged upon Jonathan Wild. Jack grasped the iron bar, which, when he had sat down, he had laid upon his knees, and stepped quickly across the room. In doing so, he had to clamber up the immense heap of bricks and rubbish which now littered the floor, amounting almost to a cartload, and reaching up nearly to the top of the chimney-piece.

Before proceeding with his task, he considered whether it would be possible to barricade the door ; but, reflecting that the bar would be an indispensable assistant in his further efforts, he abandoned the idea, and determined to rely implicitly on that good fortune which had hitherto attended him on similar occasions.

Having once more got into the chimney, he climbed to a level with the ward above, and recommenced operations as vigorously as before. He was now aided with a powerful implement, with which he soon contrived to make a hole in the wall.

The ward into which Jack was endeavoring to break was called *The Red Room*, from the circumstance of its walls having once been painted in that color ; all traces of which had, however, long since disappeared. Like *The Castle*, which it resembled in all respects, *The Red Room* was reserved for state-prisoners, and had not been occupied since the year 1716, when the gaol, as has before been mentioned, was crowded by the Preston rebels.

Having made a hole in the wall sufficiently large to pass through, Jack first tossed the bar into the room, and then crept after it.

In stepping across the room, some sharp point in the floor pierced his foot, and stooping to examine it, he found that the wound had been inflicted by a long rusty nail, which projected from the boards. Totally disregarding the pain, he picked up the nail, and reserved it for future use. Nor was he long in making it available.

On examining the door, he found it secured by a large rusty lock, which he endeavored to pick with the nail he had just acquired ; but all his efforts proving ineffectual, he removed the plate that covered it with the bar, and with his finger contrived to draw back the bolt.

Opening the door he then stepped into a narrow back passage, leading, as he was well aware, to *The Chapel*. On the left there were doors communicating with the King's Bench Ward and the Stone Ward, two large holds on the Master Debtors' side. But Jack was too well versed in the geography of the place to attempt either of them. Indeed if he had been ignorant of it, the sound of voices which he could faintly distinguish, would have served as a caution to him.

Hurrying on, his progress was soon checked by a strong door, several inches in thickness, and nearly as wide as the passage. Running his hands carefully over it in search of the lock, he perceived to his dismay it was fastened on the other side. After several vain attempts to burst it open, he resolved, as a last alternative, to break through the wall in the part nearest to the lock. This was a much more serious task than he anticipated. The wall was of considerable thickness, and built altogether of stone ; and the noise he was compelled to make in using the heavy bar, which brought sparks with every splinter he struck off, was so great, that he feared it must be heard by the prisoners on the Debtors' side. Heedless, however, of the consequences, he pursued his task.

Half an hour's labor, during which he was obliged more than once to pause

W.Clark, lith. 20 Little Bell Court

Published by J. Glover, Water Lane Fleet Street

R.

Sᵗ GILES'S BOWL.

to regain breath, sufficed to make a hole wide enough to allow a passage for his arm up to the elbow. In this way he was able to force back a ponderous bolt from its socket ; and, to his unspeakable joy, found that the door instantly yielded.

Situated at the upper part of the south-east angle of the gaol, the chapel of Old Newgate was divided into three grated compartments, or pens as they were termed, allotted to the common debtors and felons. In the north-west angle, there was a small pen for female offenders, and, on the south, a more commodious inclosure appropriated to the master debtors and strangers. Immediately beneath the pulpit stood a large circular pew where malefactors under sentence of death sat to hear the condemned sermon delivered to them, and where they formed a public spectacle to the crowds, which curiosity generally attracted on those occasions.

Jack got into one of the pens at the north side of the chapel. The enclosure by which it was surrounded was about twelve feet high ; the under part being composed of oaken planks, the upper of a strong iron grating, surmounted by sharp iron spikes. In the middle there was a gate. It was locked. But Jack speedily burst it open with the iron bar.

On one side of the chapel there was a large grated window, but, as it looked upon the interior of the gaol, Jack preferred following the course he had originally decided upon to making any attempt at this quarter.

Accordingly, he proceeded to a gate which stood upon the south, and guarded the passage communicating with the leads. It was grated and crested with spikes, like that he had just burst open, and thinking it a needless waste of time to force it, he broke off one of the spikes, which he carried with him for further purposes, and then climbed over it.

A short flight of steps brought him to a dark passage, into which he plunged. Here he found another strong door, making the fifth he had encountered. Well aware that the doors in this passage were much stronger than those in the entry he had just quitted, he was neither surprised nor dismayed to find it fastened by a lock of unusual size. After repeatedly trying to remove the plate, which was so firmly screwed down that it resisted all his efforts, and vainly attempting to pick it with the spike and nail ; he, at length, after half an hour's ineffectual labor, wrenched off the box by means of the iron bar, and the door gave way.

But this difficulty was only overcome to be succeeded by one still greater. Hastening along the passage he came to the sixth door. For this he was prepared ; but he was not prepared for the almost insurmountable obstacles which it presented. Running his hand hastily over it, he was startled to find it one complicated mass of bolts and bars. It seemed as if all the precautions previously taken were here accumulated. Any one less courageous than himself would have abandoned the attempt from a conviction of its utter hopelessness; but, though it might for a moment damp his ardor, it could not deter him.

Once again, he passed his hand over the surface, and carefully noted all the obstacles. There was a lock, apparently more than a foot wide, strongly plated, and girded to the door with thick iron hoops. Below it was a prodigiously large bolt shot into the socket, and, in order to keep it there, was fastened by a hasp, and further protected by an immense padlock. Besides this, the door was crossed and recrossed by iron bars, clenched by broad-headed nails. A strong fillet secured the socket of the bolt and the box of the lock to the main post of the doorway.

Nothing disheartened by this survey, Jack set to work upon the lock, which he attacked with all his implements,—now attempting to pick it with the nail; —now to wrench it off with the bar; but all without effect. He not only failed in making any impression, but seemed to increase the difficulties, for after an hour's toil he had broken the nail, and slightly bent the iron bar.

On reflection, it occurred to him that he might, perhaps, be able to loosen the fillet; a notion no sooner conceived than executed. With incredible labor and by the aid of both spike and nail, he succeeded in getting the point of the bar beneath the fillet. Exerting all his energies, and using the bar as a lever, he forced off the band, which was full seven feet high, seven inches wide, and two thick, and which brought with it in its fall the box of the lock, leaving no further hinderance.

Overjoyed beyond measure at having vanquished this apparently insurmountable obstacle, Jack darted through the door.

Ascending a short flight of steps, Jack found at the summit a door, which being bolted in the inside he speedily opened.

The fresh air, which blew in his face, greatly revived him. He had now reached what was called the Lower Leads,—a flat, covering a part of the prison contiguous to the gateway, and surrounded on all sides by walls about fourteen feet high. On the north stood the battlements of one of the towers of the gate. On this side a flight of wooden steps, protected by a hand-rail, led to a door opening upon the summit of the prison. This door was crested with spikes, and guarded on the right by a bristling semi-circle of spikes. Hastily ascending these steps, Jack found the door, as he anticipated, locked. He could have easily forced it, but preferred a more expeditious mode of reaching the roof which suggested itself to him. Mounting the door he had last opened, he placed his hands on the wall above, and quickly drew himself up.

Just as he got on the roof of the prison, the clock struck eight. Jack had thus been six hours in accomplishing his arduous task.

Though nearly dark, there was still light enough left to enable him to discern surrounding objects. Through the gloom he distinctly perceived the dome of St. Paul's, hanging like a black cloud in the air. As he gazed down into the courts of the prison, he could not help shuddering, lest a false step might precipitate him below.

Proceeding along the wall, Jack reached the southern tower, over the battlements of which he clambered, and crossing it, dropped upon the roof of the gate. He then scaled the northern tower, and made his way to the summit of that part of the prison which fronted Giltspur-street. Arrived at the extremity of the building, he found that it overlooked the flat-roof of a house which, as far as he could judge in the darkness, lay at a depth of twenty feet below.

Not choosing to hazard so great a fall, Jack turned to examine the building, to see whether any more favorable point of descent presented itself, but could discover nothing but steep walls, without a single available projection. As he looked around, he beheld an incessant stream of passengers hurrying on below.

Finding it impossible to descend on any side without incurring serious risk, Jack resolved to return for his blanket, by the help of which he felt certain of accomplishing a safe landing on the roof of the house in Giltspur-street.

Accordingly, he began to retrace his steps, and pursuing the course he had recently taken, scaling the two towers, and passing along the wall of the prison, he descended by means of the door upon the Lower Leads. Before he re-entered the prison, he hesitated, from a doubt whether he was not fearfully increasing his risk of capture; but, convinced that he had no other alternative, he went on.

During all this time, he had never quitted the iron bar, and he now grasped it with the firm determination of selling his life dearly, if he met with any opposition. A few seconds sufficed to clear the passage, through which it had previously cost him more than two hours to force his way. The floor was strewn with screws, nails, fragments of wood, and stone. He did not disturb any of this litter, but left it as a mark of his prowess.

He was now at the entrance of the chapel, and striking the door over which he had previously climbed a violent blow with the bar, it flew open. To vault over the pews was the work of a moment; and having gained the entry lead-ing to the *Red Room* he passed through the first door; his progress being only impeded by the pile of broken stones, which he himself had raised.

Entering the Red Room, he crept through the hole in the wall, descended the chimney, and arrived once more in his old place of captivity.

The vast heap of rubbish on the floor had been so materially increased by the bricks and plaster thrown down in his attack upon the wall of the Red Room, that it was with some difficulty he could find his blanket, which was almost buried beneath the pile. He next searched for his stockings and shoes, and when found, put them on.

Throwing the blanket over his left arm, and shouldering the iron bar, he again clambered up the chimney; regained the *Red Room;* hurried along the first passage; crossed *The Chapel;* threaded the entry to the Lower Leads; and, in less than ten minutes after quitting *The Castle,* had reached the north-ern extremity of the prison.

Previously to his descent, he had left the nail and spike on the wall, and with these he fastened the blanket to the stone coping. This done, he let him-self carefully down by it, and having only a few feet to drop, alighted in safety. Having now fairly got out of Newgate for the second time, with a heart throb-bing with exultation, he hastened to make good his escape. To his great joy he found a small garret-door in the roof of the opposite house open. He en-tered it; crossed the room, in which there was only a small truckle-bed, over which he stumbled; opened another door and gained the stair head. As he descended his chains slightly rattled. "Oh, lud! what's that?" exclaimed a female voice, from an adjoining room. "Only the dog," replied the rough tones of a man.

Securing the chain in the best way he could, Jack then hurried down the stairs, reached the lobby, and passed into the street.

And thus he was once more free, having effected one of the most wonderful escapes ever planned or accomplished.

Published by J. Glover, Water Lane, Fleet St.

W. Clerk, lith. 20, High Holborn.

S.

THE ARRIVAL AT TYBURN.

CHAPTER XXII.

THE PURSUIT.

UNDER an impression that his safety would be more certain in the country than the town, Jack bent his steps towards the suburbs, carrying with him the iron bar which had done so much good service in his grand escape.

To avoid observation from the passers, who still filled the larger thoroughfares, Jack threaded his way through bye lanes and alleys. If he succeeded in reaching the open country, he felt assured of making good his escape. With this object he pursued his course at a rapid pace, until he met with an obstacle as unlooked-for as it was unwelcome.

On emerging from an alley near Holborn Bridge, Jack Sheppard came full upon a figure which he at once recognised to be his inveterate foe, Jonathan Wild!

The recognition was mutual; and after a vacant stare of wonder, the thief-taker recovered himself sufficiently to exclaim in a voice of thunder, "Jack Sheppard! Out of Newgate! damnation!"

Although amazed at the meeting, Sheppard darted past; and before Jonathan had power to seize him, had placed some distance between himself and his enemy, which, being a much lighter man he continued to improve in the chase that was immediately commenced.

"After him! After him!" cried Wild. "It is Jack Sheppard, he has broken out of Newgate—a hundred pounds to the man who takes him." And with his best speed he followed the unfortunate fugitive.

A watchman whose box was placed against the churchyard wall, near the entrance to Shoe Lane, rushed out and sprung his rattle, which was immediately answered by another rattle from Holborn Bars.

Darting down Field Lane, Jack struck into a labyrinth of streets on the left; but though he ran as swiftly as he could, he was not unperceived. His course had been observed by the watchman, who directed Wild which way to take.

Sheppard's name operated like magic on the crowd. The cry was echoed

No. 18.]

S

by twenty different voices.   People ran out of their shops to join the pursuit ;
and, by the time Wild had got into Field Lane, he had a troop of fifty persons
at his heels—all eager to assist in the capture.

"Stop thief!" roared Jonathan, who perceived the fugitive hurrying along a
street towards Hatton Garden.   "It is Sheppard—Jack Sheppard—stop him!"
And his shouts were reiterated by the pack of blood-hounds at his heels.

Jack, meanwhile, heard the shouts, and, though alarmed by them, held on a
steady course.   By various twistings and turnings, during all which time his
pursuers, who were greatly increased in numbers, kept him in view, he
reached Grays-Inn Lane.   Here he was hotly pursued.   Fatigued by his previous exertions, and incumbered by his fetters, he was by no means—though
ordinarily remarkably swift of foot—a match for his foes, who were fast gain-
ing upon him.

"Stop thief!" roared Jonathan.   "Stop thief!" clamored the rabble behind.

At no loss to comprehend that Jack was the individual pointed out by these
outcries, several made a dash at him.   But Jack eluded their grasp.   A large
dog was set at him by a stable boy ; but, striking the animal with his faithful
iron bar, he speedily sent him yelping back.   But Jack, whose strength began
to fail, feared he could not hold out much longer.   Determined, however, not
to be taken with life, he held on.

Still keeping ahead of his pursuers, he ran along the direct road, till the
houses disappeared, and he got into the open country.   Here he was preparing to leap over the hedge into the fields on the left, when he was intercepted
by two horsemen, who, hearing the shouts, rode up and struck at him with the
butt-ends of their heavy riding whips.   Warding off the blows as well as he
could with the bar, Jack struck both the horses on the head, and the animals
plunged so violently, that they not only prevented their riders from assailing
him, but also kept off the hostlers ; and, in the confusion that ensued, Jack
managed to spring over the fence, and shaped his course across the fields.

The stoppage had materially lessened the distance between him and his pursuers, who now amounted to more than a hundred persons, many of whom carried lanterns and links.   Ascertaining that it was Sheppard of whom this concourse was in pursuit, the two horsemen leapt the hedge, and were presently
close upon him.   Like a hare closely pressed, Jack attempted to double, but
the device only brought him nearer his foes, who were crossing the field in
every direction, and rending the air with their shouts.   The uproar was tremendous—men yelling—dogs barking,—but above all was heard the stentorian
voice of Jonathan, urging them on.   Jack was so harassed that he felt half
inclined to stand at bay.

While he was straining every sinew, his foot slipped, and he fell, head foremost, into a deep trench, which he had not observed in the dark. This fall saved him, for the horsemen passed over him. Creeping along quickly on his hands and knees, he found the entrance to a covered drain, into which he crept. He was scarcely concealed when he heard the horsemen, who perceived they had overshot their mark, ride back.

By this time, Jonathan and the vast mob attending him, had come up, and the place was rendered almost as light as day by the links.

"He must be somewhere hereabouts," cried one of the horsemen, dismounting. "We were close upon him when he suddenly disappeared."

Jonathan made no answer, but snatching a torch from a bystander, jumped into the trench, and commenced a diligent search. Just as he had arrived at the mouth of the drain, and Jack felt certain he must be discovered, a loud shout was raised from the further end of the field that the fugitive was caught. All the assemblage, accompanied by Jonathan, set off in this direction, when it turned out that the supposed housebreaker was a harmless beggar, who had been found asleep under a hedge.

Jonathan's vexation at the disappointment was expressed in the bitterest imprecations, and he returned as speedily as he could to the trench. But he had now lost the precise spot; and thinking he had examined the drain, turned his attention to another quarter.

Meanwhile, the excitement of the chase had in some degree subsided. The crowd dispersed in different directions, and most fortunately a heavy shower coming on, put them altogether to flight. Jonathan, however, still lingered. He seemed wholly insensible to the rain, though it presently descended in torrents, and continued in search as ardently as before.

After occupying himself thus for the best part of an hour, he thought Jack must have given him the slip. And with a mortified look he unwillingly left the spot.

About an hour after this, Jack ventured to emerge from his place of concealment. It was still raining heavily, and profoundly dark. Drenched to the skin,—in fact, he had been lying in a bed of muddy water,—and chilled to the very bone, he felt so stiff, that he could scarcely move.

Without an idea where he was going, Jack pursued his way through the fields; and, as he proceeded, the numbness of his limbs in some degree wore off, and his confidence returned, He had need of all the inexhaustible energy of his character to support him through his toilsome walk over the wet grass, or along the slippery ploughed land. At last, he got into a lane, but had not proceeded far when he was again alarmed by the sound of a horse's tread.

Once more breaking through the hedge he took to the fields. He was now almost driven to despair. Wet as he was, he felt if he lay down in the grass, he should perish with cold; while, if he sought a night's lodging in any asylum, his dress, stained with blood and covered with dirt, would infallibly cause him to be secured and delivered into the hands of justice. And then the fetters, which were still upon his legs:—how was he to get rid of them?

Tired and dispirited, he still wandered on. Again returning to the main road, he passed through Clapton; and turning off on the left, he arrived at the foot of Stamford Hill. He walked on for an hour longer, till he could scarcely drag one leg after another. At length, he fell down on the road, fully expecting each moment would prove his last.

How long he continued thus he scarcely knew: but just before dawn, he managed to regain his legs, and, crawling up a bank, perceived he was within a quarter of a mile of Tottenham. A short way off in the fields he descried a sort of shed or cow-house, and thither he contrived to drag his weary limbs. Opening the door, he found it littered with straw, on which he threw himself, and instantly fell asleep.

When he awoke it was late in the day, and raining heavily. For some time he could not stir, but felt sick and exhausted. His legs were dreadfully swelled; his hands bruised; and his fetters occasioned him intolerable pain. Rousing himself, he went to the door. It had ceased raining, but the atmosphere was thick and chill, and the ground deluged by the recent showers. Taking up a couple of large stones which lay near, Jack tried to beat the round basils of the fetters into an oval form, so as to enable him to slip his heels through them.

On examining his pockets he found about twenty guineas in gold, and some silver. But how to avail himself of it was the question, for in his present garb he was sure to be recognized. When night fell, he crept into the town of Tottenham. As he passed along the main thoroughfare, he heard his own name pronounced, and found it was a hawker, crying a penny history of his escapes. A crowd was collected round the fellow, who was rapidly disposing of his stock.

Further on, there was a small chandler's shop, where, seeing provisions in the window, Jack ventured in and bought a loaf. Having secured this,— for he was almost famished,—he said that he had lost a hammer and wished to purchase one. The old woman told him she had no such article to dispose of, but recommended him to a neighboring blacksmith.

Guided by the glare of the forge, which threw a stream of ruddy light across

JACK SHEPPARD'S DEATH.

Published by J. Glover, Water Lane, Fleet St.

W. Clerk. lith. 201 High Holborn

the road, Jack soon found the place of which he was in search. Entering the workshop, he found the blacksmith occupied in heating the tire of a cart-wheel. Suspending his labor on Jack's appearance, the man demanded his business. Making up a similar story to that which he had told the old woman, he said he wanted to purchase a hammer and a file.

The man looked hard at him.

"Answer me one question first," he said; "I half suspect you're Jack Sheppard.

"I am," replied Jack, without hesitation; for he felt assured from the man's manner that he might confide in him.

"You're a bold fellow, Jack," rejoined the blacksmith. "But you've done well to trust me. I'll take off your irons—for I guess that's the reason why you want the hammer and file—on one condition."

"What is it?"

"That you give 'em to me."

"Readily."

Taking Jack into a shed behind the workshop, the smith in a short time freed him from his fetters. He not only did this, but supplied him with an ointment which allayed the swelling of his limbs, and crowned all by furnishing him with a jug of excellent ale.

"I'm afraid, Jack, you'll come to the gallows," observed the smith; "but if you do, I'll go to Tyburn to see you. But I'll never part with your irons."

Noticing the draggled condition Jack was in, he then fetched him a bucket of water, with which Jack cleansed himself as well as he could, and thanking the honest smith, who would take nothing for his trouble, left the shop.

Having made a tolerably good meal upon the loaf, overcome by fatigue, Jack turned into a barn in Stoke Newington, and slept till late in the day, when he awakened much refreshed. The swelling in his limbs had also subsided. It rained heavily all day, so he did not stir forth.

Towards night, however, he ventured out, and walked on towards London. When he arrived at Hoxton, he found the walls covered with placards, offering a reward for his apprehension, and he everywhere appeared to be the general subject of conversation. From a knot of idlers at a public-house, he learnt that Jonathan Wild had just ridden past, and that his setters were scouring ne country in every direction.

Destiny seemed to decree Jack's career as about to close; for after passing the night in rambling from place to place in the hope of meeting Edgeworth Bess he ventured at day break to approach her lodgings.

He approached stealthily, and knocked at the door; which after a little delay was opened, and he darted into the house; but instead of the welcome he anticipated from Bess, he was pounced upon by four men, and securely bound, in a manner that rendered even a show of resistance fruitless.

It appeared that Jonathan Wild had relied on the probability of Jack's visiting Edgeworth Bess, from the love which he knew they bore each other, and had stationed officers in the house to seize him if he should appear.

Edgeworth Bess had been prevented leaving her lodgings by order of Wild, and the state of mind in which she waited, after hearing of Jack's escape, and knowing the trap that was prepared for him should he venture to seek an asylum with her, was indescribable. Sleep had forsaken her eyelids since she had endured the fear that her lover would be entrapped through his affection for her : and when she heard the scuffle in the passage caused by the entry of Jack, she flew down stairs, and beheld him in the hands of the officers, who soon bound him hand and foot.

Bess had sufficient self possession to know that any expression of alarm or terror from her, must augment the sufferings of Sheppard ; she, therefore, in a forced strain of bravado, exclaimed, " Courage! courage, dear Jack, and you shall yet conquer : go back to Newgate; but be assured, they shall never take you to Tyburn. " We'll save you yet, Jack—be of good heart : " she then threw herself beside her lover, who was lying in the passage securely bound completely disconcerted at the suddenness of his capture, and, clasping her arms around his neck, passionately kissed him.

The officers were not however disposed to allow any waste of time and rudely separating their charge from the grasp of Edgeworth Bess, hurried him off to Newgate with a taunt, that if he escaped again, he should retain his liberty unmolested.

CHAPTER XXIII.

THE LAST!

JACK's career now drew towards its close. Loaded with the heaviest fetters, and constantly watched by two of the gaolers' assistants, who neither quitted him for a single moment, nor suffered any visitor to approach him, he found all attempts to escape impracticable.

On Thursday, the 12th of November, after having endured nearly a month's imprisonment, Jack was conveyed from Newgate to Westminster Hall. He was placed in a coach, handcuffed, and heavily fettered, and guarded by a vast posse of officers to Temple Bar, where a fresh relay of constables escorted him to Westminster.

Arrived in the Hall, the prisoner's handcuffs were removed, and he was taken before the Court of King's Bench. The record of his conviction at the Old Bailey sessions was then read; and as no objection was then offered to it, the Attorney-General moved that his execution might take place on Monday next.

As the day appointed for the execution was now close at hand, the prisoner, who seemed to have abandoned all hopes of escape, turned his thoughts entirely from worldly considerations.

The morning of Monday the 16th of November 1724 at length dawned. It was a dull, foggy day, and the atmosphere was so thick and heavy, that, at eight o'clock, the curious who arrived near the prison could scarcely discern the tower of St Sepulchre's church.

By and by the tramp of horses' feet was heard slowly ascending Snow Hill, and presently a troop of grenadier guards rode into the area facing Newgate. These were presently joined by a regiment of foot. A large body of the constables of Westminster next made their appearance, the chief of whom entered the Lodge, where they were speedily joined by the civic authorities. At nine o'clock, the sheriffs arrived, followed by their officers and javelin-men.

At this moment, the Bell of Newgate began to toll, and was answered by another bell from St Sepulchre's. The great door of the Stone Hall was thrown open, and the sheriffs, preceded by the javelin-men, entered the room. They were followed by Jonathan Wild, who carried a stout stick under his arm, and planted himself near the stone. Not a word was uttered by the assemblage ; but a hush of expectation reigned throughout.

Another door was next opened, and, preceded by the ordinary, with the sacred volume in his hand, the prisoner entered the room. Though encumbered by his irons, his step was firm, and his demeanor dignified. His countenance was pale as death, but not a muscle quivered ; nor did he betray the slightest appearance of fear. On the contrary, it was impossible to look at him without perceiving that his resolution was unshaken.

Advancing with a slow firm step to the stone-block, he placed his left foot upon it, drew himself up to his full height, and fixed a look so stern upon Wild, that the thieftaker quailed before it.

The prison smith, meantime, began to ply his hammer, and speedily unriveted the chains. The first stroke appeared to arouse all the vindictive passions of Jonathan. Fixing a ferocious and exulting look upon Jack Sheppard, he exclaimed,

" At length, my vengeance is complete."

" Wretch !" cried Jack, " your triumph will be short-lived. Before a year has expired, you will share the same fate."

" If I do, I care not," rejoined Wild : " I shall have lived to see you hanged."

Every preparation had been made outside for the prisoner's departure. At the end of two long lines of foot-guards stood the cart with a powerful horse harnessed to it. At the head of the cart was placed the coffin. On the right were several mounted grenadiers : on the left, some half dozen javelin-men.

The first person who issued from the lodge was the hangman, who proceeded to the cart, and took his seat upon the coffin.

A deep silence now prevailed, broken only by the tolling of the bells of Newgate and St Sepulchre's. The mighty concourse became for a moment still. Suddenly, such a shout as has seldom smitten human ears, rent the air. " He comes !" cried a thousand voices, and the shout ascended to Smithfield, descended to Snow Hill, and told those who were assembled on Holborn Hill that Sheppard had left the prison.

Between two officers, with their arms linked in his, Jack Sheppard was conducted to the cart. He looked around, and as he heard that deafening shout, —as he felt the influence of those thousand eyes fixed upon him—as he listened to the cheers, all his misgivings, if he had any, vanished, and he felt

Published by F. Glover, Water Lane, Fleet St.

W. Clark, lith, 202 High Holborn

JACK SHEPPARD.

more as if he were marching to a triumph, than proceeding to a shameful death.

Jack had no sooner taken his place in the cart, than he was followed by the ordinary, who seated himself beside him, and, opening the book of prayer, began to read aloud. Excited by the scene, Jack, however could pay little attention to the good man's discourse, and was lost in a whirl of tumultuous emotions.

The cavalcade was now put slowly in motion. The horse-soldiers wheeled round and cleared the path: the foot closed in upon the cart. Then came the javelin-men, walking four abreast, and, lastly, a long line of constables, marching in the same order.

Slowly descending Snow-Hill, the train passed on its way, attended by the same stunning vociferations, cheers, yells, and outcries, which had accompanied it on starting from Newgate. The guards had great difficulty in preserving a clear passage without resorting to severe measures, for the tide, which poured upon them behind, around, in front, and at all sides, was almost irresistible. The houses on Snow Hill were thronged, like those in the Old Bailey. Every window, from the ground floor to the garret had its occupant, and the roofs were covered with spectators. Words of encouragement and sympathy were addressed to Jack, who, as he looked around, beheld many a friendly glance fixed upon him.

In this way, they reached Holborn Bridge. Here a little delay occurred. The passage was so narrow that there was only sufficient room for the cart to pass, with a single line of foot-soldiers on one side ; and, as the walls of the bridge were covered with spectators, it was not deemed prudent to cross it till these persons were dislodged.

The advanced guard rode on to drive away any opposition, while the main body of the procession crossed the bridge, and slowly toiled up Holborn Hill.

The object of all this, never altered his position, but sat back in the cart as if resolved not to make even a struggle to regain his liberty.

The procession now wound its way without further interruption along Holborn. Like a river swollen with many currents, it gathered force from the various avenues that poured their streams into it.

At length, the train approached St Giles's. Here according to an old custom, a criminal taken to execution was allowed to halt at a tavern, called the Crown, and take a draught from The St Giles's Bowl, " as his last refreshment on earth." At the door of this tavern, which was situated on the left of the street not more than a hundred yards distant from the church, the bell of which began to toll as soon as the procession came in sight, the cart drew up, and the whole cavalcade halted. A wooden balcony in one of the adjoining houses was thronged with ladies, all of whom appeared to take a lively interest in the scene, and to be full of commiseration for the criminal, not, perhaps, unmixed with admiration of his appearance.

A scene now ensued, highly characteristic of the age, and the occasion. The doleful procession at once assumed a festive character. Many of the soldiers dismounted, and called for drink. Their example was immediately imitated by the officers, constables, javelin men, and other attendants ; and nothing was to be heard but shouts of laughter and jesting,—nothing seen but the passing of glasses, and the emptying of foaming jugs. The hangman, very composedly filled and lighted his pipe.

At this moment, the landlord of the Crown, a jovial-looking stout personage, with a white apron round his waist, issued from the house, bearing a large wooden bowl filled with ale, which he offered to Jack, who instantly rose to receive it. Raising the bowl in his right hand, Jack glanced towards the group of ladies, and begged to drink their health ; he then turned to the others, who extended their hands towards him, and raised it to his lips.

Once again the cavalcade was in motion, and winding its way by St Giles's church, the bell of which continued tolling all the time, passed the pound, and entered Oxford Road, or, as it was then not unfrequently termed, Tyburn Road. After passing Tottenham Court Road, very few houses were to be seen on the right hand, and opposite Wardour Street it was open country.

The crowd now dispersed amongst the fields, and thousands of persons were seen hurrying towards Tyburn as fast as their legs could carry them, leaping over hedges, and breaking down every impediment in their course.

Besides those who conducted themselves more peaceably, the conductors of the procession noticed with considerable uneasiness, large bands of men armed with staves, bludgeons, and other weapons, who were flying across the fields in the same direction. As it was feared that some mischief would ensue, it was thought proper that a small body of men, should ride forward to Tyburn, and keep the ground clear until the arrival of the prisoner.

This suggestion was instantly acted upon, and a body of the grenadiers rode forward.

The train, meantime, had passed Mary-le-bone Lane, when it again paused for a moment, at Jack's request.

Scarcely had it come to a halt, when a stalwart man, in spite of opposition, offered his large horny hand to the prisoner. Jack instantly recognised the honest blacksmith, who had freed him from his irons at Tottenham.

"I am here, you see," said the smith, as he grasped Jack's hand, and gave it a hearty shake; "I told you I would come and bid you farewell."

Accept my hearty thanks," replied Jack, returning the salutation; "farewell! In a few minutes all will be over."

The smith turned aside to hide the tears that started to his eyes,—for with a man's courage, he still had a woman's heart.

Tyburn was now at hand. Over the sea of heads arose a black and dismal object. It was the gallows. Jack, whose back was towards it, did not see it; but he heard, from the pitying exclamations of the crowd, that it was in view. This circumstance produced no further alteration in his demeanor, except that he endeavored to abstract himself from the surrounding scene, and bend his attention to the prayers which the ordinary was reciting.

A deep dread calm, like that which precedes a thunder-storm, now prevailed amongst the assemblage. The thousand voices which a few moments before had been so clamorous, were now hushed. Not a breath was drawn. The troops had kept a large space clear around the gallows. The galleries adjoining it were crowded with spectators,—so was the roof of a large tavern, then the only house standing at the end of the Edgeware Road,—so were the trees,—the walls of Hyde Park,—a neighboring barn, a shed,—in short, every available position.

The cart, meanwhile, had approached the fatal tree. The guards, horse and foot, and constables, formed a wide circle round it to keep off the mob. It was an awful moment—so awful, that every other feeling except deep interest in the scene seemed suspended.

At this terrible juncture, Jack maintained his composure,—a smile played upon his face before the cap was drawn over it,—and the last words he uttered were, "My poor mother! I shall soon join her!" The rope was then adjusted and the cart began to move.

The next instant, he was launched into eternity!

Scarcely had he been turned off a moment, when the mob made a tremendous rush towards the gallows—their leader leapt into the cart with an open clasp knife in his hand, and, before he could be prevented, cut down the body. At the same instant, a volley of musketry poured from the guards, bringing down the foremost of the rabble, and sending several bullets into the yet breathing body of Jack Sheppard.

The most conspicuous figure in this *emente* was Edgeworth Bess, who, by the most energetic action encouraged the mob

Jack's body was caught, and passed from hand to hand over a thousand heads, until it was far from the fatal tree. The body was conveyed to a room engaged by Edgeworth Bess, and carefully examined. It had been cut down before life was extinct, but the bullets of the soldiery had pierced his heart !

Thus died Jack Sheppard !!!

Various accounts are extant of the burial place of the housebreaker ; but, in the doubt which must continue to exist, we can only offer the most probable. Two days after the foregoing incident, Mrs Sheppard's grave in Willesden churchyard was opened, for another burial. One person alone, besides the clergyman and sexton, attended the ceremony. It was a female, who appeared deeply affected. The coffin was lowered into the earth, but the mourner remained to weep ; shortly after a neat white stone was placed at the head of the grave, simply bearing the initials

www.ingramcontent.com/pod-product-compliance
Lightning Source LLC
Chambersburg PA
CBHW081155170626
46813CB00009B/3194